Palace of the Peacock

Palace of the Peacock

WILSON HARRIS

FABER AND FABER
3 Queen Square
London

First published in 1960
by Faber and Faber Limited
3 Queen Square London W.C.1
First published in this edition 1968
Reprinted 1973 and 1977
Printed in Great Britain by
Whitstable Litho Ltd Whitstable Kent

ISBN 0 571 08930 5

For

Margaret, Nigel and Sydney

It ceases to be history and becomes . . . fabricated for pleasure, as moderns say, but I say by Inspiration.

BLAKE

And after the earthquake a fire; but the Lord was not in the fire: and after the fire a still small voice.

I KINGS xix, 12

Preface

I

Palace of the Peacock (1960) is the first of seven novels[1] published to date by Wilson Harris. The author (b. 1921) now lives in London where his works are written, but his novels grow out of his responsiveness to the brooding continental landscape and the fabulous fragmented history of his native Guyana (formerly British Guiana). The declaration of the dreaming, half-blinded narrator of *Palace of the Peacock* might well serve as an epigraph: "They were an actual stage, a presence, however mythical they seemed to the universal and the spiritual eye. They were as close to me as my ribs, the rivers and the flatland, the mountains and heartland I intimately saw. I could not help cherishing my symbolic map, and my bodily prejudice like a well-known room and house of superstition within which I dwelt. I saw this kingdom of man turned into a colony and battleground of spirit, a priceless tempting jewel I dreamed I possessed" (p. 20). Harris's fiction brings imperial/slave history and the aftermath into its field, but the author's way of seeing the world around him and kind of fiction in which it expresses itself challenge us to see with new eyes.

In "Tradition and the West Indian Novel",[2] a lecture of 1964, Harris used the term "novel of persuasion" to suggest the mainstream tradition of the English nineteenth-century novel. "The novel of persuasion rests on grounds of apparent common sense: a certain 'selection' is made by the writer, the selection of

[1] The next six are: *The Far Journey of Oudin* (1961); *The Whole Armour* (1962); *The Secret Ladder* (1963); *Heartland* (1964); *The Eye of the Scarecrow* (1965); and *The Waiting Room* (1967).

[2] Published in a collection of critical essays by Harris, *Tradition, the Writer and Society*, New Beacon Publications (1967).

items, manners, uniform conversation, historical situations, etc., all lending themselves to build and present an individual span of life which yields self-conscious and fashionable judgments, self-conscious and fashionable moralities. The tension which emerges is the tension of individuals—great or small—on an accepted plane of society we are persuaded has an inevitable existence." The Guyanese writer's practice in *The Far Journey of Oudin* helps us to understand these contentions better. In this novel, Harris makes use of the East Indian presence, but he does not chronicle "an individual span of life" in the way in which, for example, V. S. Naipaul traces the life and death of Mohun Biswas in *A House for Mr Biswas* (1961). And whereas Naipaul's relentless accumulation of realistic particulars from the social scene persuades us and the character that that society has "an inevitable existence", Harris's fiction suggests a particular society only to deny its overpowering and absolute quality. Superficially, *The Far Journey of Oudin* is a witty analogy of slave history: Oudin, the landless, harbourless, jack-of-all-trades of the empty savannah is a tool used by both sides in the struggle between old (the Mohammed estate) and new economic forces (the money-lender, Ram). Since the novel opens with the death of Oudin, there is an initial temptation to think of it in terms of "flashback". But as the work unfolds, through apparently unrelated incidents and with arbitrary shifts in point of view, it begins to emerge that Oudin's death is only a device to remove a conventional view of the deprived character. Two versions of Oudin's life take shape: there is the socially realistic figure who suffers as a slave in an oppressive social order, and who dies having covenanted even his unborn child to the grasping Ram; and there is the god-like inheritor of the kingdom who fulfils destiny by abducting the virgin Beti, a bride and prize coveted by Ram. The two Oudins are evoked with equal credibility, both stories residing in the same events. Like Blake in the two "Holy Thursday" poems, Harris shows and responds to the coexistence of different conditions—the meek being overwhelmed by the earth, but inheriting it at the same time. Through imaginative fictions it is possible to remember that no social order is inevitable and ultimate, and that the "individual span of life" need not be identified with the most oppressive of its possibilities. But "the novel of persuasion", Harris might argue, with its commitment to ordinary linear time, to the creation of finite characters and to the portrayal of a self-sufficient social world with reference to which characters are valued, indulges a one-sided view of human life, a restricted vision of human capacities.

Harris's disregard for the usual conventions (time, character, social realism) in the novel arises from an almost literal-minded obsession with expressing intuitions about "the person" and about the structure of societies men have built for themselves through the ages. He sees these intuitions, however, as being of particular and immediate concern in the West Indies. At the beginning of "Tradition and the West Indian Novel" he finds remarkable in the West Indian "a sense of subtle links, the series of subtle links which are latent within him, the latent ground of old and new personalities". Harris would hardly imagine this to be an exclusive West Indian property, but such a conception of the person seems natural in the West Indies where so many different cultures and peoples have interacted on each other. Instead of creating characters whose positioning on one side or other of the region's historical conflicts consolidates those conflicts and does violence to the make-up of the person, the West Indian novelist should set out to "visualize a fulfilment", a reconciliation in the person and throughout society, of the parts of a heritage of broken cultures.

It is for these reasons that Toussaint L'Ouverture is such an important figure for Harris. C. L. R. James's *The Black Jacobins* (1938) is "a severe and imaginative reconstruction of the historical figure, Toussaint L'Ouverture—Africa, the Caribbean, Europe", but Harris is not satisfied with James's explanations of Toussaint's uncertainties—his hesitation to declare Haiti sovereign and independent, his ambivalent attitude to the Frenchman Sonthonax and to his European diplomatic contacts, his equivocal dealings with his black generals, and his alienation from his extreme followers. For Harris, the "uncertainty of design" in Toussaint's mind after the revolution, indicated "a groping towards an alternative to conventional statehood, a conception of wider possibilities and relationships which still remains unfulfilled today in the Caribbean". James's failure to contain Toussaint in the historical frame allows Harris to recognize in the black revolutionary's fluid constitution the need for "a profound and difficult vision of the person—a profound and difficult vision of essential unity within the most bitter forms of latent and active historical diversity". A vision of essential unity is pervasive in Harris's fiction, taking different forms from novel to novel. This vision and "a conception of wider possibilities and relationships which still remains unfulfilled today in the Caribbean" are the special substance of *The Whole Armour*, Harris's most obviously political novel to date.

With *The Secret Ladder* and *Heartland*, Harris begins a concentrated exploration of "the person". The peasant types of the earlier works are replaced by central characters who are servants of modern technology—educated, articulate and introspective. In each novel there is a confrontation with an ancestral figure (Poseidon the ancient African in *The Secret Ladder* and Petra the pregnant promiscuous Amerindian in *Heartland*). Poseidon is the agent through whom Fenwick becomes aware of man's frailty and eternal endurance in an overwhelming universe; and through Petra, Stevenson experiences the possibility of rebirth and self-discovery. But above all it is in contact with the primeval jungle (always a disconcerting element in Harris's novels, but coming into its own as a prime agent here) that both Fenwick and Stevenson lose themselves as particular men in a specific social and historical context. Both novels end in disorientation. Although it is possible to follow Fenwick and Stevenson as we follow characters in conventional novels, Harris has no interest in his central figures as individuals. It was necessary to begin with solid, clearly defined and self-sufficient characters in order to dramatize their breakdown. What Harris is trying to do in these novels is to create a sense of man's original condition of terror and freedom prior to the accretions of history and civilization.

The significance of this movement in Harris's oeuvre and its relation to his view of the possibilities in the West Indian situation become clearer in *The Eye of the Scarecrow* and *The Waiting Room* which open with characters in that emptied out condition on the edge of self-discovery with which *The Secret Ladder* and

Heartland end. In *The Waiting Room*, a blind woman, convalescing after a series of operations, sits like a statue in a room full of antiques and relics of her past. There is little authorial direction, the language is dense and involuted, and the narrative yields itself fragmentarily. But it is apparent that through a process of memory of which she is not in full control, Susan Forrestal is reliving her unfinished affair with a rapacious lover she had dismissed in the past. As the disjointed memories of her absent lover float into the woman's consciousness, the reader becomes aware that the statuesque person, the inanimate relics in the room and the absent lover are bound together in the waiting room, in the way that the enthralled Ulysses was bound to the saving mast while his crew moved free on the deck below, their ears, however, deafened to the Sirens. Such a distribution of strengths and weaknesses between animate and inanimate objects in the room allows for a relayed digestion of the whole catastrophe while offering mutual protection from its annihilating powers.

So the ground of loss or deprivation with which most West Indian writers and historians engage is not for Harris simply a ground for protest, recrimination and satire; it is visualized through the agents in his works as an ambivalent condition of helplessness and self-discovery, the starting point for new social structures. By the time that *The Waiting Room* comes to be written, Harris's exploration of this condition in the person has gone so far that the personal relationship—violent rape, irresponsible lover, involuntarily responsive mistress learning to digest catastrophe—absorbs the burden of an equally rapacious imperial relationship. Susan Forrestal, blind, helpless, and deprived, involved in the waiting room in the development of new resources and capacities for relationships with people and things, becomes the exciting ambivalent emblem of a so-called "hopeless", "historyless" West Indian condition.

II

Each of Harris's novels stands by itself. But their effects are cumulative; more particularly, a reading of the first five novels makes it less difficult to enter into the species of fiction Harris invents in the sixth and seventh. To read the novels serially, in order of publication, moreover, is to experience the unpredictable movements and deepening implications in Harris's explorations of the same basic elements: the essential unity of man in spite of historical diversity and historical conflicts; the capacity of the person to endure and to respond, however involuntarily, "to the essence of life, to the instinctive grains of life which continue striving and working in the imagination for fulfilment"; and the sense of a Caribbean cultural and physical environment charged with witnesses and relics of both of these as they await realization in a particular society. *Palace of the Peacock* contains all Harris's basic themes, and anticipates his later designs. It is the rounded poetic vision which he proceeds to translate into everyday life in the novels that follow.

III

At the end of *Palace of the Peacock*, the I-narrator with whose dreams and nightmares the work began, breaks out of finite existence into a timeless ecstatic sphere: "One was what I am in the music—buoyed up and supported above dreams by the undivided soul and anima in the universe from whom the word of dance and creation first came . . .". Harris's gifts as an imaginative writer make this the credible and convincing climax to a novel rather than a mystic's appeal to the faith and agreement of his fellow-believers. For even at this moment of apotheosis, Harris's sense of the genuine human impossibility of breaking through for more than the visionary moment (and this is also the tact of the novelist) dictates that the dream should fade. What is left is the human paradox that generates the tension in all Harris's novels: "Each of us now held at last in his arms what he had been for ever seeking and what he had eternally possessed."

The extractable story of the novel is straightforward enough. A boat's crew beats its way up-river through the Guyanese jungles and rapids towards an Amerindian settlement called Mariella, only to find that the folk have fled. The crew discover an old Amerindian woman lurking about in the deserted village, force her to act as their guide, and set off in pursuit of the folk. During the hazardous journey beyond Mariella, violence breaks out among the crew, a natural death occurs and there is accidental death by drowning. On the seventh day they drift into the presence of a massive waterfall at the source of the river. Here the boat is wrecked and the rest of the crew meet their deaths.

The recognizable basis of the story is the European pursuit of gold and the Indians in the sixteenth and seventeenth centuries. This is rapidly complicated. In the first place, Harris's sense of man's essential unity does not allow him to reconstruct the historical conflict between invader and invaded. The crew heading up-river towards Mariella is led by Donne, a type of Elizabethan adventurer and conquistador, and is made up of the descendants and mixtures of peoples—Europeans, Africans, Portuguese, Indians—belonging historically to different centuries and to successive waves of migrants to the Caribbean. And Harris invents for them a complicated and incestuous family tree that is highly credible to readers aware of Caribbean history or the history of the American South. The crew, moreover, is a replica of a famous crew that had been drowned on a similar exploiting mission some time before, and they not only shuttle between life and death at their author's arbitrary demands, they are burdened by their complex ghost in the form of concrete memories and premonitions of disaster and futility in their earthly lives. There are further complications: as they are accompanied by the inhibited I-narrator whose dreams reveal an obsessive identification with Donne and Donne's imperial lust, it is not possible to make out whether the crew exist independently or are merely creatures of the dreamer's free imagination. The characters are difficult to hold on to, not because they exist in different times and in different mental and physical states, but because the vividness and energy with which Harris makes them inhabit each fragment defeats our attempts to discover a key that will allow us to settle that one state is "real" while the others are illusory. It is Harris's purpose, in fact, to suggest the interaction of all these levels of man's existence at one and the same time.

The use of epigraphs from Blake, Yeats, Donne, the Bible and Hopkins; and the division of the novel into four books are the most obvious evidence of design in *Palace of the Peacock*. In Book I, Harris suggests the repetitive and eventually cynical toil of living and dying without fulfilment that is human existence trapped in the historic moment (the "repetitive boat and prison of life"). At the same time, however, in the energy with which different races and individuals in history return to the quest, and in the continued urgings of dream, imagination, memory and premonition, the author seeks to recognize all men's instinctive (primordial) longing for and uncanny knowledge of an ultimate satisfaction (see p. 34, "In this remarkable filtered light . . . Vigilance's spirit"). This is how it comes about that Harris can challenge the flat historical view of the European invasions, and see the spirit's quest subsisting on memory, even in the sordid frustrated episode recounted in the novel. (A particular illustration of this and of Harris's imaginative prose at its whitest heat occurs on pp. 71–3 when the crew with an Amerindian woman in their midst drift into the straits of memory.)

After the "cruelty and confusion" and "the blindness and frustration of desire" in Book I, Book II "The Mission of Mariella" shows the lifting of the masks of self-sufficiency, cynicism and stoicism that the members of the crew had learnt to wear. (See especially the narrator's nightmares, pp. 45–6 and Donne's vacillation "I saw that Donne . . . laughed and cried", pp. 54–61.) In Book III, "The Second Death", begins the seven-day creative journey beyond Mariella (earthly hopes), the journey in which the deaths of the crew are enacted singly and with certain sacrificial overtones. Finally in Book IV, the crew, freed of their fetishes climb laboriously up the ladders on the sides of a waterfall where they have visions, sensuously rendered in the novel, of the divine creator and healer (pp. 131–7, a modification of the Cosmic Tree) and of a frail brilliant mother and child (pp. 137–9, the Mother of the Earth). The I-narrator returns to describe the constellation of the crew and their ecstasy, and as the visions fade he comments on the paradox of all their existence: "Each of us now held at last in his arms what he had been for ever seeking and what he had eternally possessed" (p. 152).

Such are the bare bones in the design. The actual reading

experience is more complex. Because its eyes are shut to the usual notions about time, character and event in the novel, *Palace of the Peacock* tends to run against the expectations of habitual readers of fiction. Its narrative technique is equally disconcerting, for although it is furnished with an I-narrator, he does little either to provide a sense of sequential development in the work or to explain its absence. Harris leaves it to the responsive reader to fill in the gaps between a series of vividly realized episodes, and to *sense,* with the whole novel behind him the ways in which the apparently unrelated parts act upon one another. For example, when the crew gaze through the window in the wall of the cliff, the dreamer's downward gaze upon the blank face and staring eye of the murdered horseman of the savannahs seems to come to mind; and at the end the dreamer's vision of "the crowded creation of the invisible savannahs" from the windows of the palace suggests a contrast with the time when from Donne's room he stared "blindly through the window at an invisible population". As with gesture, episode and event, so with language: Harris's far-fetched similes and grotesque metaphors, his forceful yoking of unlikely words and his breathless sentences invite us to respond sensuously before seeking an intellectual ordering: "Tiny embroideries resembling the handwork on the Arawak woman's kerchief and the wrinkles on her brow turned to incredible and fast soundless breakers of foam. Her crumpled bosom and river grew agitated with desire, bottling and shaking every fear and inhibition and outcry. The ruffles in the water were her dress rolling and rising to embrace the crew. This sudden insolence of soul rose and caught them from the powder of her eyes and the age of her smile and the dust in her hair all flowing back upon them with silent streaming majesty and abnormal youth and in a wave of freedom and strength" (p. 73). In *Palace of the Peacock*, Harris contracts out of the "novel of persuasion". The reader is excitingly invited to trust his senses and to immerse himself in the imaginative substance of the work.

KENNETH RAMCHAND

August 1968
University of Kent at Canterbury

Contents

BOOK I

Horseman, Pass By

Cast a cold eye
On Life, on death.
Horseman, pass by.

YEATS

1

A horseman appeared on the road coming at a breakneck stride. A shot rang out suddenly, near and yet far as if the wind had been stretched and torn and had started coiling and running in an instant. The horseman stiffened with a devil's smile, and the horse reared, grinning fiendishly and snapping at the reins. The horseman gave a bow to heaven like a hanging man to his executioner, and rolled from his saddle on to the ground.

The shot had pulled me up and stifled my own heart in heaven. I started walking suddenly and approached the man on the ground. His hair lay on his forehead. Someone was watching us from the trees and bushes that clustered the side of the road. Watching me as I bent down and looked at the man whose open eyes stared at the sky through his long hanging hair. The sun blinded and ruled my living sight but the dead man's eye remained open and obstinate and clear.

I dreamt I awoke with one dead seeing eye and one

living closed eye. I put my dreaming feet on the ground in a room that oppressed me as though I stood in an operating theatre, or a maternity ward, or I felt suddenly, the glaring cell of a prisoner who had been sentenced to die. I arose with a violent giddiness and leaned on a huge rocking-chair. I remembered the first time I had entered this bare curious room; the house stood high and alone in the flat brooding countryside. I had felt the wind rocking me with the oldest uncertainty and desire in the world, the desire to govern or be governed, rule or be ruled for ever.

Someone rapped on the door of my cell and room. I started on seeing the dream-horseman, tall and spare and hard-looking as ever. "Good morning," he growled slapping a dead leg and limb. I greeted him as one greeting one's gaoler and ruler. And we looked through the window of the room together as though through his dead seeing material eye, rather than through my living closed spiritual eye, upon the primitive road and the savannahs dotted with sentinel trees and slowly moving animals.

His name was Donne, and it had always possessed a cruel glory for me. His wild exploits had governed my imagination from childhood. In the end he had been expelled from school.

He left me a year later to join a team of ranchers near the Brazil frontier and border country. I learnt then to fend for myself and he soon turned into a ghost, a million dreaming miles away from the sea-coast where we had lived.

"The woman still sleeping," Donne growled, rapping on the ground hard with his leg again to rouse me from my inner contemplation and slumber.

"What woman?" I dreamed, roused to a half-waking sense of pleasure mingled with foreboding.

"Damnation," Donne said in a fury, surveying a dozen cages in the yard, all open. The chickens spied us and they came half-running, half-flying, pecking still at each other piteously and murderously.

"Mariella," Donne shouted. Then in a still more insistent angry voice—"Mariella".

I followed his eyes and realized he was addressing a little shack partly hidden in a clump of trees.

Someone was emerging from the shack and out of the trees. She was barefoot and she bent forward to feed the chickens. I saw the back of her knees and the fine beautiful grain of her flesh. Donne looked at her as at a larger and equally senseless creature whom he governed and ruled like a fowl.

I half-woke for the second or third time to the sound of insistent thumping and sobbing in the hall outside my door. I awoke and dressed quickly. Mariella stood in the hall, dishevelled as ever, beating her hand on my door.

"Quiet, quiet," I said roughly, shrinking from her appearance. She shuddered and sobbed. "He beat me," she burst out at last. She lifted her dress to show me her legs. I stroked the firm beauty of her flesh and touched the ugly marks where she had been whipped. "Look," she said, and lifted her dress still higher. Her convulsive sobbing stopped when I touched her again.

A brilliant day. The sun smote me as I descended the steps. We walked to the curious high swinging gate like a waving symbol and warning taller than a hanging man whose toes almost touched the ground; the gate was as curious and arresting as the prison house we had left above and behind, standing on the tallest stilts in the world.

"Donne cruel and mad," Mariella cried. She was staring hard at me. I turned away from her black hypnotic eyes as if I had been blinded by the sun, and saw inwardly in the haze of my blind eye a watching muse and phantom whose breath was on my lips.

She remained close to me and the fury of her voice was in the wind. I turned away and leaned heavily against the frail brilliant gallows-gate of the sky, looking down upon the very road where I had seen the wild horse, and the equally wild demon and horseman fall. Mariella had killed him.

I awoke in full and in earnest with the sun's blinding light and muse in my eye. My brother had just entered the room. I felt the enormous relief one experiences after a haze and a dream. "You're still alive," I cried involuntarily. "I dreamt Mariella ambushed and shot you." I started rubbing the vision from my eye. "I've been here just a few days," I spoke guardedly, "and I don't know all the circumstances"—I raised myself on my elbow—"but you are a devil with that woman. You're driving her mad."

Donne's face clouded and cleared instantly. "Dreamer," he warned, giving me a light wooden tap on the shoulder, "life here is tough. One has to be a devil to survive. I'm the last landlord. I tell you I fight everything in nature, flood, drought, chicken hawk, rat, beast and woman. I'm everything. Midwife, yes, doctor, yes, gaoler, judge, hangman, every blasted thing to the labouring people. Look man, look outside again. Primitive. Every boundary line is a myth. No-man's land, understand?"

"There are still labouring people about, you admit that." I was at a loss for words and I stared blindly through the window at an invisible population.

"It's an old dream," I plucked up the courage to express my inner thoughts.

"What is?"

"It started when we were at school, I imagine. Then you went away suddenly. It stopped then. I had a curious sense of hard-won freedom when you had gone. Then to my astonishment, long after, it came again. But this time with a new striking menace that flung you from your horse. You fell and died instantly, and yet you were the one who saw, and I was the one who was blind. Did I ever write and tell you"—I shrank from Donne's supercilious smile, and hastened to justify myself—"that I am actually going blind in one eye?" I was gratified by his sudden startled expression.

"Blind?" he cried.

"My left eye has an incurable infection," I declared. "My right eye—which is actually sound—goes blind in my dream," I felt foolishly distressed. "Nothing kills *your* sight," I added with musing envy. "And your vision becomes," I hastened to complete my story, "your vision becomes the only remaining window on the world for me."

I felt a mounting sense of distress.

"Mariella?" There was a curious edge of mockery and interest in Donne's voice.

"I never saw her before in my dream," I said. I continued with a forced warmth—"I am glad we are together again after so many years. I may be able to free myself of this—this—" I searched for a word—"this obsession. After all it's childish."

Donne flicked ash and tobacco upon the floor. I could see a certain calculation in his dead seeing eye. "I had almost forgotten I had a brother like you," he smiled matter-of-factly. "It had passed from my mind —this dreaming twin responsibility you remember." His voice expanded and a sinister under-current ran through his remarks—"We belong to a short-lived family and people. It's so easy to succumb and die. It's the usual thing in this country as you well know." He was smiling and indifferent. "Our parents died early. They had a hard life. Tried to fight their way up out of an economic nightmare: farmers and hand-to-mouth business folk they were. They gave up the ghost before they had well started to live." He stared at me significantly. "I looked after you, son." He gave me one of his ruthless taps. "Father and Mother rolled into one for a while. I was a boy then. I had almost forgotten. Now I'm a man. I've learnt," he waved his hands at the savannahs, "to rule *this*. This is the ultimate. This is everlasting. One doesn't have to see deeper than that, does one?" He stared at me hard as death. "Rule the land," he said, "while you still have a ghost of a chance. And you rule the world. Look at the sun." His dead eye blinded mine. "Look at the sun," he cried in a stamping terrible voice.

2

The map of the savannahs was a dream. The names Brazil and Guiana were colonial conventions I had known from childhood. I clung to them now as to a curious necessary stone and footing, even in my dream, the ground I knew I must not relinquish. They were an actual stage, a presence, however mythical they seemed to the universal and the spiritual eye. They were as close to me as my ribs, the rivers and the flatland, the mountains and heartland I intimately saw. I could not help cherishing my symbolic map, and my bodily prejudice like a well-known room and house of superstition within which I dwelt. I saw this kingdom of man turned into a colony and battleground of spirit, a priceless tempting jewel I dreamed I possessed.

I pored over the map of the sun my brother had given me. The river of the savannahs wound its way far into the distance until it had forgotten the open land. The dense dreaming jungle and forest emerged. Mariella dwelt above the falls in the forest. I saw the rocks bristling in the legend of the river. On all sides the falling water boiled and hissed and roared. The rocks in the tide flashed their presentiment in the sun, everlasting courage and the other obscure spirits of creation. One's mind was a chaos of sensation, even pleasure, faced by imminent mortal danger. A white fury and foam churned and raced on the black tide that grew golden every now and then like the crystal memory of sugar. From every quarter a mindless stream came through the ominous rocks whose presence served to pit the mad foaming face. The boat shuddered in an anxious grip and in a living streaming hand that issued from the bowels of earth. We stood on the threshold of a precarious standstill. The outboard engine and propeller still revolved and flashed with mental silent horror now that its roar had been drowned in other wilder unnatural voices whose violent din rose from beneath our feet in the waters. Donne gave a louder cry at last, human and incredible and clear, and the boatcrew sprang to divine attention. They seized every paddle and with immortal effort edged the vessel forward. Our bow pointed to a solid flat stone unbroken and clear, running far into the river's bank. It looked near and yet was as far from us as the blue sky from the earth. Sharp peaks and broken hillocks grew on its every side, save where we approached, and to lose our course or fail to keep our head signified a crashing stop with a rock boring and gaping open our bottom and side. Every man paddled and sweated and strained toward the stone and heaven in his heart. The bowman sprang upon the hospitable ground at last followed by a nimble pair from the crew. Ropes were extended and we were drawn into a pond and still water between the whirling stream and the river's stone.

I felt an illogical disappointment and regret that we were temporarily out of danger. Like a shell after an ecstasy of roaring water and of fast rocks appearing to move and swim again, and yet still and bound as ever where the foam forced its way and seethed and curdled and rushed.

The crew swarmed like upright spiders, half-naked, scrambling under a burden of cargo they were carrying ashore. First I picked and counted the da-Silva twins of Sorrow Hill, thin, long-legged, fair-skinned, of Portuguese extraction. Then I spotted old Schomburgh, also of Sorrow Hill, agile and swift as a monkey for all his seasoned years. Donne prized Schomburgh as a bowman, the best in all the world his epitaph boasted and read. There was Vigilance, black-haired, Indian, sparkling and shrewd of eye, reading the river's mysterious book. Vigilance had recommended Carroll, his cousin, a thick-set young Negro boy gifted with his paddle as if it were a violin and a sword together in paradise. My eye fell on Cameron, brick-red face, slow feet, faster than a snake in the forest with his hands; and Jennings, the mechanic, young, solemn-featured, carved out of still wood it seemed, sweating still the dew of his tears, cursing and reproving his whirling engine and toy in the unearthly terrifying grip in the water. Lastly I counted Wishrop, assistant bowman and captain's understudy. Wishrop resembled Donne, especially when they stood side by side at the captain's paddle. I felt my heart come into my mouth with a sense of recognition and fear. Apart from this fleeting wishful resemblance it suddenly seemed to me I had never known Donne in the past—his face was a dead blank. I saw him now for the first faceless time as the captain and unnatural soul of heaven's dream; he was myself standing outside of me while I stood inside of him.

The crew began, all together, tugging and hauling the boat, and their sing-song cry rattled in my throat. They were as clear and matter-of-fact as the stone we had reached. It was the best crew any man could find in these parts to cross the falls towards the Mission where Mariella lived. The odd fact existed of course that their living names matched the names of a famous dead crew that had sunk in the rapids and been drowned to a man, leaving their names inscribed on Sorrow Hill which stood at the foot of the falls. But this in no way interfered with their lifelike appearance and spirit and energy. Such a dreaming coincidence we were beginning to learn to take in our stride. Trust Donne to rake up every ghost in his hanging world and house. Mariella was the obsession we must encounter at all costs, and we needed gifted souls in our crew. Donne smiled with a trace of mockery at my rank impatience. His smile suddenly changed. His face grew younger and brutal and impatient too. And innocent like a reflection of everlasting dreaming life.

The sun was high in the heavens. The river burned and flamed. The particular section, where we were, demanded hauling our vessel out of the water and along the bank until we had cleared an impassable fury and obstruction. The bright mist lifted a little from my mind's eye, and I saw with a thumping impossible heart I was reliving Donne's first innocent voyage and excursion into the interior country. This was long before he had established himself in his brooding hanging house. Long before he had conquered and crushed the region he ruled, annihilating everyone and devouring himself in turn. I had been struck by a peculiar feeling of absence of living persons in the savannahs where he governed. I knew there were labouring people about but it had seemed that apart from his mistress—the woman Mariella—there was no one anywhere. Now she too had become an enigma; Donne could never hope to regain the affection and loyalty he had mastered in her in the early time when he had first seduced her above the doom of the river and the waterfall. Though he was the last to admit it, he was glad for a chance to return to that first muse and journey when Mariella had existed like a shaft of fantastical shapely dust in the sun, a fleshly shadow in his consciousness. This had vanished. And with his miraculous return to his heart's image and lust again, I saw—rising out of the grave of my blindness—the nucleus of that bodily crew of labouring men I had looked for in vain in his republic and kingdom. They had all come to me at last in a flash to fulfil one self-same early desire and need in all of us.

I knew I was dreaming no longer in the way I had been blind and dreaming before. My eye was open and clear as in the strength of youth. I stood on my curious stone as upon the reality of an unchanging presence Donne had apprehended in a wild and cruel devouring way which had turned Mariella into a vulgar musing executioner. This vision and end I had dimly guessed at as a child, fascinated and repelled by his company as by the company of my sleeping life. How could I escape the enormous ancestral and twin fantasy of death-in-life and life-in-death? It was impossible to turn back now and leave the crew in the wild inverse stream of beginning to live again in a hot and mad pursuit in the midst of imprisoning land and water and ambushing forest and wood.

The crew—all of us to a man—toiled with the vessel to lift it from still water and whirlpool. At last it stood on the flat stone. We placed round logs of wood beneath it, and half-rolled, half-pushed, until its bow poked the bushy fringe on the bank. This was the signal for reconnoitre. A wild visionary prospect. The sun glowed upon a mass of vegetation that swarmed in crevices of rocky nature until the stone yielded and turned a green spongy carpet out of which emerged enormous trunks and trees from the hidden dark earth beneath and beyond the sun.

The solid wall of trees was filled with ancient blocks of shadow and with gleaming hinges of light. Wind rustled the leafy curtains through which masks of living beard dangled as low as the water and the sun. My living eye was stunned by inversions of the brilliancy and the gloom of the forest in a deception and hollow and socket. We had armed ourselves with prospecting knives and were clearing a line as near to the river as we could.

The voice of roaring water declined a little. We were skirting a high outcrop of rock that forced us into the bush. A sigh swept out of the gloom of the trees, unlike any human sound as a mask is unlike flesh and blood. The unearthly, half-gentle, half-shuddering whisper ran along the tips of graven leaves. Nothing appeared to stir. And then the whole forest quivered and sighed and shook with violent instantaneous relief in a throaty clamour of waters as we approached the river again.

We had finished our connection, and we began retracing our steps in the line to the starting point where our boat stood. I stopped for an instant overwhelmed by a renewed force of consciousness of the hot spirit and moving spell in the tropical undergrowth. Spider's web dangled in a shaft of sun, clothing my arms with subtle threads as I brushed upon it. The whispering trees spun their leaves to a sudden fall wherein the ground seemed to grow lighter in my mind and to move to meet them in the air. The carpet on which I stood had an uncertain place within splintered and timeless roots whose fibre was stone in the tremulous ground. I lowered my head a little, blind almost, and began forcing a new path into the trees away from the river's opening and side.

A brittle moss and carpet appeared underfoot, a dry pond and stream whose course and reflection and image had been stamped for ever like the breathless outline of a dreaming skeleton in the earth. The trees rose around me into upward flying limbs when I screwed my eyes to stare from underneath above. At last I lifted my head into a normal position. The heavy undergrowth had lightened. The forest rustled and rippled with a sigh and ubiquitous step. I stopped dead where I was, frightened for no reason whatever. The step near me stopped and stood still. I stared around me wildly, in surprise and terror, and my body grew faint and trembling as a woman's or a child's. I gave a loud ambushed cry which was no more than an echo of myself—a breaking and grotesque voice, man and boy, age and youth speaking together. I recovered myself from my dead faint supported by old Schomburgh, on one hand, and Carroll, the young Negro boy, on the other. I was speechless and ashamed that they had had to come searching for me, and had found me in such a state.

Schomburgh spoke in an old man's querulous, almost fearful voice, older than his fifty-odd seasoned years. Words came to him with grave difficulty. He had schooled himself into a condition of silent stoical fear that passed for rare courage. He had schooled himself to keep his own counsel, to fish in difficult waters, to bow or steer his vessel under the blinding sun and the cunning stars. He spoke now out of necessity, querulous, scratching the white unshaven growth on his chin.

"Is a risk everyman tekking in this bush," he champed his mouth a little, rasping and coughing out of his lungs the old scarred broken words of his life. I thought of the sound a boat makes grating against a rock. "Is a dead risk," he said as he supported me. "How you feeling son?" he had turned and was addressing me.

Carroll saw my difficulty and answered. "Fine, fine," he cried with a laugh. His voice was rich and musical and young. Schomburgh grinned, seasoned, apologetic, a little unhappy, seeing through the rich boyish mask. Carroll trembled a little. I felt his work-hardened hands, so accustomed to abnormal labour they always quivered with a muscular tension beyond their years; accustomed to making a tramp's bed in the bottom of a boat and upon the hard ground of the world's night. This toughness and strength and enduring sense of limb were a nervous bundle of longing.

"Fine, fine," he cried again. And then his lively eyes began darting everywhere, seeking eagerly to forget himself and to distract his own thoughts. He pointed—"You notice them tracks on the ground Uncle? Game plenty-plenty."

Old Schomburgh scratched his bearded chin. "How you feeling?" he rasped at me again like a man who stood by his duty.

"Fine, fine, right as rain Uncle," Carroll cried and laughed. Old Schomburgh turned his seasoned apology and grin on Carroll—almost with disapproval I felt—"How come you answer so quick-quick for another man? You think you know what mek a man tick? You can't even know you own self, Boy. You really think you can know he or me?" It was a long speech he had made. Carroll trembled, I thought, and faltered a little. But seeing the difficulty I still had in replying, he cried impulsively and naively taking words from my lips—"He fine-fine Uncle, I tell you. I know—"

"Well why he so tongue-tied?"

"He see something," Carroll laughed good-naturedly and half-musingly, staring once again intently on the ground at the tracks he had discerned.

Schomburgh was a little startled. He rubbed away a bit of grey mucus from the corners of his eyes. His expression grew animal-sharp and strained to attention. Every word froze on his lips with the uncanny silence and patience of a fisherman whose obsession has grown into something more than a normal catch. He glared into my eye as if he peered into a stream and mirror, and he grumbled his oldest need and desire for reassurance and life. He caught himself at last looking secretive and ashamed that he had listened to what Carroll had said. I too started suddenly. I felt I must deny the vague suggestion—given as an excuse to justify my former appearance and stupefaction—that I had seen something. I was about to speak indignantly when I saw the old man's avid eye fixed shamefully on me, and felt Carroll's labouring hand tremble with the longing need of the hunter whose vision leads him; even when it turns faint in the sense of death. I stifled my words and leaned over the ground to confirm the musing foot-fall and image I had seen and heard in my mind in the immortal chase of love on the brittle earth.

3

It took us three days to take to the river again and launch our boat after hauling it through the open line we had cut. The rapids appeared less dangerous before and after us. It was Vigilance who made us see how treacherous they still were. We had been travelling for several hours when he gave a shrill warning cry, pointing with his finger ten yards ahead of the bow. I detected a pale smooth patch that seemed hardly worth a thought. It was the size of the moon's reflection in streaming water save that the moment I saw it was broad daylight. The river hastened everywhere around it. Formidable lips breathed in the open running atmosphere to flatter it, many a wreathed countenance to conceal it and half-breasted body, mysterious and pregnant with creation, armed with every cunning abortion and dream of infancy to claim it. Clear fictions of imperious rock they were in the long rippling water of the river; they condescended to kneel and sit, half-turning away from, half-inclining and bending towards the pale moon patch of death which spun before them calm as a musical disc. Captain and bowman heeded Vigilance's cry turning to momentary stone like the river's ruling prayer and rock. They bowed and steered in the nick of time away from the evasive, faintly discernible unconscious head whose meek moon-patch heralded corrugations and thorns and spears we dimly saw in a volcanic and turbulent bosom of water. We swept onward, every eye now peeled and crucified with Vigilance. The silent faces and lips raised out of the heart of the stream glanced at us. They presented no obvious danger and difficulty once we detected them beneath and above and in our own curious distraction and musing reflection in the water.

It was a day of filtered sunshine, half-cloud, half-sun. Wishrop had been bowing for old Schomburgh. He retired to the stern of the vessel to relieve Donne who looked the strangest shadow of himself, falling across the boat into the water, I suddenly thought. The change in Donne I suddenly felt in the quickest flash was in me. It was something in the open air as well, in the strange half-sun, in the river, in the forest, in the mysterious youthful longing which the whole crew possessed for Mariella and for the Mission where she lived above the falls. The murdered horseman of the savannahs, the skeleton footfall on the river bank and in the bush, the moonhead and crucifixion in the waterfall and in the river were over as though a cruel ambush of soul had partly lifted its veil and face to show that death was the shadow of a dream. In this remarkable filtered light it was not men of vain flesh and blood I saw toiling laboriously and meaninglessly, but active ghosts whose labour was indeed a flitting shadow over their shoulders as living men would don raiment and cast it off in turn to fulfil the simplest necessity of being. Wishrop was an excellent steersman. The boat swayed and moved harmoniously with every inclination of his body upon the great paddle. A lull fell upon the crew, transforming them, as it had changed Donne, into the drumming current of the outboard engine and of the rapid swirling water around every shadowy stone. All understanding flowed into Wishrop's dreaming eternity, all essence and desire and direction, wished-for and longed-for since the beginning of time, or else focused itself in the eye of Vigilance's spirit.

In this light it was as if the light of all past days and nights on earth had vanished. It was the first breaking dawn of the light of our soul.

BOOK II

The Mission of Mariella

. . . the widow-making unchilding unfathering deeps.

HOPKINS

4

Our arrival at the Mission was a day of curious consternation and belief for the colony. The news flew like lightning across the river and into the bush. It seemed to fall from the sky through the cloudy trees that arched high in the air and barely touched, leaving the narrowest ribbon of space. The stream that reflected the news was inexpressibly smooth and true, and the leaves that sprinkled the news from the heavens of the forest stood on a shell of expectant water as if they floated half on the air, half on a stone.

We drove at a walking pace through the brooding reflecting carpet unable to make up our minds where we actually stood. We had hardly turned into the bank when a fleet of canoes devoured us. Faces pressed upon us from land and water. The news was confirmed like wild-fire. We were the news. It was ourselves who were the news. Everyone remembered that not so long ago this self-same crew had been drowned to a man in the rapids below the Mission. Everyone recalled the visits the crew had paid the

Mission from time to time leading to the fatal accident. They recalled the event as one would see a bubble, bright and clear as the sun, bursting unexpectedly and knitting itself together again into a feature of sheer consternation, mingled gladness and fear. Or into a teardrop, sadness and unexpected joy running together, in the eye of a friend or a woman or a child.

They did not know how to trust their own emotion, almost on the verge of doubting the stream in their midst. Old Schomburgh looked as timeless as every member of the crew. Carroll, Vigilance, Wishrop, the daSilva twins. The wooden-faced, solemn-looking Jennings stood under the disc and toy that had spun the grave propeller of the world. Where there had been death was now the reflection of life.

The unexpected image of Donne awoke a quiver of sudden alarm and fright. A heavy shadow fell upon all of us—upon the Mission, the trees, the wind, the water. It was an ominous and disturbing symptom of retiring gloom and darkened understanding under the narrow chink and ribbon of sky. They shrank from us as from a superstition of dead men. Donne had had a bad name in the savannahs, and Mariella, to their dreaming knowledge, had been abused and ill-treated by him, and had ultimately killed him. Their faces turned into a wall around her. She was a living fugitive from the devil's rule. This was the birth and beginning of a new fantasy and material difficulty and opposition.

We had barely succeeded in tying our boat securely to the bank than they had left us alone. We could see their houses— set down in little clearings —through the trees. The small thatched walls and sloping roofs were made of cocerite palm—a sure sign of goodness and prosperity. The flesh of the cocerite fruit was succulent and dreamy and white, and the tree only appeared where there was promising land.

The young children playing and scrambling near the cocerite houses had vanished with the entire population, and the Mission now looked abandoned.

"We sleeping in a funny-funny place tonight," Wishrop said wonderingly.

"Them Buck folk scare of dead people bad-bad," Cameron laughed, chewing a sweet blade of grass. "They done know all-you rise bodily from the grave. Big frauds! that is what all you is." He spoke with affection.

His face was brick-red as the first day we had set out, his hair close and curling and negroid. His hands moved like a panther boxing and dancing and quick, and in a moment he had slung his hammock between the trees near the river's edge. He sat in it and tested it, rocking awhile. His brow and expression endorsed the sureness and the life in his hands. They bore an air of patience and experience, a little tired and cynical almost one would imagine when he smiled and his face wrinkled a little: a timeless long-suffering wrinkle of humour and scepticism and native poetry that knew the guts of the world wherein had been invested and planted the toughest breed of sensibility time had ever known.

Cameron's great-grandfather had been a dour Scot, and his great-grandmother an African slave and mistress. Cameron was related to Schomburgh (whom he addressed as Uncle with the other members of the crew) and it was well-known that Schomburgh's great-grandfather had come from Germany, and his' great-grandmother was an Arawak American Indian. The whole crew was one spiritual family living and dying together in a common grave out of which they had sprung again from the same soul and womb as it were. They were all knotted and bound together in the enormous bruised head of Cameron's ancestry and nature as in the white unshaven head of Schomburgh's age and presence.

It was this thread of toughness and guts that Cameron understood and revelled in more than any other man. It gave him his slowness and caution of foot (in contradistinction to the speed in his hands):

he stood like a melodramatic rock in mother earth, born from a close fantasy and web of slave and concubine and free, out of one complex womb, from a phantom of voluptuousness whose memory was bitter and rebellious as death and sweet as life; every discipline and endurance and pain he felt he knew. But this boast sprang from a thriftless love of romance and a genuine optimism and self-advertisement and self-ignorance.

Cynicism and ribaldry were the gimmick he adopted. Courage was native and spontaneous. Stoicism and shame played a minor part in fashioning his consciousness of himself and his adopted wrinkle and mask. He was never a cunning fisherman like Schomburgh, straining his attention upon the fish that swam in the river, only to delude himself after a while about the nature of his catch. Cameron knew in as plain and literal terms as hell fire itself what it was he actually wanted and had never been able to gain.

He wanted space and freedom to use his own hands in order to make his own primitive home and kingdom on earth, hands that would rule everything, magical hands dispensing life and death to their subjects as a witch doctor would or a tribal god and judge. This was a gross exaggeration of his desires and intentions, an enormous extension and day-dream to which hard and strong and tough men are curiously subject though they fear and seek to reprove themselves for thinking in such a light. In fact it was the only unconscious foreboding (in the midst of his affections and laughter) Cameron ever experienced, the closest he came to Schomburgh's guilt and imagination he dimly felt to lie beyond his years. So it was, unwitting and ignorant, he had been drawn to his death with the others, and had acquired the extraordinary defensive blindness, ribald as hell and witchcraft, of dying again and again to the world and still bobbing up once more lusting for an ultimate satisfaction and a cynical truth.

There was always the inevitable Woman (he had learnt to capitalize his affairs)—the anchor that tied him down for a while against his will and exercised him into regaining his habitual toughness to break away again for good. Still he could never scrape together enough money—after every grotesque adventure—to buy the place he wanted. That was the taste of death and hell: to make do always with another unintelligent and seedy alternative, while the intelligent and fruitful thing remained just beyond his grasp.

"A miss is as good as a mile," he sang aloud impishly. "I must scrape together some real capital—" he winked his eye at the company. "The soil here good", he spoke stoutly. "Right here in this Mission is the start I always seeing in view. Donkey's years I seeing it I tell you. I never seem to quite make it you know. Maybe I'm silly in the upper mental story of me house,"—he tapped his head humbly. "Not smart and obliging enough. Fact is we don't speak the same language that is God's truth. They speak shy and tricky—the Mission folk. I speak them hard bitter style of words I been picking up all me life. Is the way I make me living." He scowled and looked at the world for approval, like a man who conceals his dread of his mistress turning into his witch and his widow. "I got to keep making these brutal sounds to live. You realize these Mission folk is the only people who got the real devil of a title to this land?" He opened his hands helplessly. "If only the right understanding missy and mistress would come along sweet and lucky and Bucky and rich, Ah would be in heaven, boys." He let his foot drag on the ground crunching the soil a little. His head swung suddenly, in spite of himself and against his will, turning an envious reflective eye on the image of Donne—a superstitious eye almost, fearing the evil within himself as the Mission folk had feared Donne within them.

"You think you really want this ghost of a chance you fishing for?" Schomburgh interrupted. "Maybe you don't understand you can drive and scare the blasted soul of the world away and lose your bait for good." It was a speech for him. He had his fishing-rod in his hands and was adjusting the line, rubbing his itching unshaven chin on his shoulders as the gloomy words broke in his chest like an ancient cough. Cameron trembled a little with a sense of cruel unwanted cold, the meaningless engagement with and stab of death that he—with the entire crew—had not yet shaken off. It was a wind blowing on the water, a knife and chill they recognized like tropical fever that blew out of the Mission in an ague of fears, shaking the leaves of the dreaming forest.

5

Night fell on curling flames, on our hammocks curling too like ash and ghost, and the trees turning black as charcoal. Fugitive green shone on the leaves nearest us in the illumination of the camp fire, turning black a little farther away on the fringe of the brittle glaring shadow reflected in the river at our feet.

The fire subsided slowly, spitting stars and sparks every now and then and barking like a hoarse dog. The burning logs crouched and settled and turned white as fur still burning all the while underneath their whiteness redly and sombrely.

The white fur greyed to hourly ash as the night aged in the trees and the fugitive fiery green of dreaming leaves turned faintly silver and grey in anticipation of the pale shadow of dawn.

It was the first night I had spent on the soil of Mariella. So it seemed to me in a kind of hallucination drawing me away from the other members of the crew. Every grey hammock around me became an empty cocoon as hollow as a deserted shell and a house.

I felt the soul of desire to abandon the world at the critical turning point of time around which curled the ash and the fur of night. I knew the keen marrow of this extreme desire and desertion, the sense of animal flight lacking true warmth, the hideous fascination of fire devoid of all burning spirit.

A dog rose and stood over me. A horse it was in the uncertain grey light, half-wolf, half-donkey, monstrous, disconsolate; neighing and barking in one breath, its terrible half-hooves raised over me to trample its premature rider. I grew conscious of its closeness as a shadow and as death. I made a frightful gesture to mount, and it shrank a little into half-woman, half-log greying into the dawn. Its teeth shone like a misty rag, and I raised my hand to cajole and stroke its ageing, soulful face. I sat bolt upright in my hammock, shouting aloud that the devil himself must fondle and mount this muse of hell and this hag, sinking back instantly, a dead man in his bed come to an involuntary climax. The grey wet dream of dawn had restored to me Mariella's terrible stripes and anguish of soul. The vaguest fire and warmth came like a bullet, flooding me, over aeons of time it seemed, with penitence and sorrow.

This musing re-enactment and reconstruction of the death of Donne ushered in the early dawn with a grey feeling inside. The leaves dripped in the entire forest the dewy cold tears of the season of drought that affected the early tropical morning and left me rigid and trembling. A pearl and half-light and arrow shot along the still veined branches. The charcoal memory of the hour lifted as a curtain rises upon the light of an eternal design. The trees were lit with stars of fire of an unchanging and perfect transparency. They hung on every sensitive leaf and twig and fell into the river, streaking the surface of the water with a darting appearance crimson as blood. It was an illusory reflection growing out of the strength of the morning light on my closed eyelids and I had no alternative but to accept my eye as a shade between me and an inviolate spirit. It seemed to me that such a glimpse of perfection was a most cruel and distressing fact in that it brought me face to face with my own enormous frailty. It grew increasingly hard to believe that this blindness and error were all my material fantasy rather than the flaw of a universal creation. For manhood's sake and estate I saw there must arise the devil of resistance and incredulity toward a grotesque muse which abandoned and killed and saved all at the same time with the power of indestructible understanding and life.

How stupid and silly to lose the cruel expectation and stronghold of death. It was the surest gamble

I had known in my life; I was mad to believe I had seen an undying action and presence in the heart-felt malice of all mystery and seduction.

How could I surrender myself to be drawn two ways at once? Indeed what a phenomenon it was to have pulled me, even in the slightest degree, away from nature's end and wish, and towards the eternal desire and spirit that charged the selfsame wish of death with shades of mediation, precept upon precept in the light of my consciousness which was in itself but another glimmering shadow hedging the vision and the glory and the light.

I awoke now completely and fully. I tried to grapple again with my night-and-morning dream; it all faded and vanished. I recognized a curious sense of inner refreshment. The old innocent expectations and the journey—Donne's first musing journey to Mariella—returned with a rush. The eccentric emotional lives of the crew every man mans and lives in his inmost ship and theatre and mind were a deep testimony of a childlike bizarre faith true to life. It was as if something had snapped again, a prison door, a chain, and a rush and flight of appearances jostled each other—past, present and future in one constantly vanishing and reappearing cloud and mist. I rubbed my eyes. Old Schomburgh was carefully cleaning the fish he had caught the night before. Cameron was poking and lighting the fire, assisted by a young man with high pale cheeks —one of the daSilva twins.

"Cammy," the young man was saying in a confidential rather duncified tone, "an old woman knocking about one of them houses. I see she since foreday morning." He pointed.

"Only she come back?" Cameron was incredulous.

"Looking so," daSilva said.

"Well what in hell really going on. . . ."

"Have you chaps seen Donne anywhere?" I interrupted from my hammock.

"He and me brother gone for a lil look-see walk," daSilva said somewhat heavily. His voice had a moody almost stupid drawl out of keeping with the slight active life of his hands and limbs.

I rose and began dressing.

"You don't think is Donne scare them away?" daSilva spoke to me confidentially.

"I dunno," I said, vaguely stirred by sleeping memories. "They're funny folk."

"But you *know* is he," daSilva insisted, repeating a brutal time-worn lesson.

"They fear *you* too," I waved my hand as vaguely as ever around.

"Yes, I s'pose so," daSilva consented heavily. "But is a different-different thing," he argued, struggling with an emotional tide. "I been to this Mission before and I can't remember me doing harm to anybody. Don't laugh, Cammy. I know I mek a chile with one of the women. I see you laughing . . ." he stopped and gave a coarse heavy bray astonishing for his frail chest and shoulders. "You mean to say" —he argued—"a man wife and chile going run from he?"

Cameron replied by laughing soundlessly.

"You got a bad name, Cammy," daSilva said, wishing to arouse in his companion a sense of shame—"such a bad name you is a marked man. All the trips you been mekking to the Mission and you just can't pick a pepper." It was his turn to laugh lugubriously and derisively.

Cameron sobered a little. "Where's there's life there's hope, Boy." He tried to jeer daSilva by giving his words a ribald drawling twist. "You lucky bastard—you." He poked daSilva in the chest. "What's in hell's name keeping you from settling right here for good?"

"You don't know what?"

"Naw Boy, I don't."

"I ain't marry to she," daSilva confessed.

"Ah see," Cameron laughed like a man who had at last dismissed his fool.

"Pon this Mission," daSilva explained in a nettled voice, "you know as well as I the law say you must marry the Bucks you breed. Nobody know is me chile."

"Is it a secret?" Cameron roared and laughed again.

"Well is an open secret," daSilva said in his heavy foolish way. "Last year when the boat hit moonhead—remember?—was the first and last time for me—I see real hell. Like if the chile real face and the mother real face all come before me. Like if even as I deading in the waterself something pulling me back. Ah mek up me mind then to do the right thing by she. . . ."

"You skull crack wide open, daSilva. Still," he sighed and mocked in one breath, "every new year is a fool's new paradise. I wish I could mek the grade meself Boy. A rich piece of land like this! And is now everybody gone and vanish."

"Is a true thing you seeing. Just vanish."

Schomburgh gave one of his hoarse brief chuckles. "They bound to vanish. They don't *see* dead people really, do they? Nor dead people seeing them for long."

"I ain't dead," Cameron cried. "I can prove it any day." He sniffed the air in which had risen the delightful smell of cooking fish.

"Uncle thinking of his epitaph," daSilva said with his slow heavy brand of humour, " 'pon Sorrow hill. You must be seen you own epitaph sometimes in your dreams, Cammy? Don't lie." He winked at

Cameron impressing upon him a conspiracy to humour the old man. Schomburgh intercepted the wink like a man who saw with the back of his head.

"I see you, daSilva," he croaked out of an intuitive omniscience. He bent over the fire and the meal he had started preparing, half-ashamed, resenting the uneasy foundations of knowledge he possessed. His uncertainty in the rescue and apprehension of being, started tears in his eyes like smoke and fearful belief all mingled together. He stood up abruptly, losing all appetite.

"Come, come, Uncle," Cameron roared and scowled. "You must try some of this ripe nice fish. Breakfast! lads! Uncle. It's good fish not the devil himself you catch."

6

Donne and the other daSilva twin returned as I put the last petrified morsel in my mouth. They were accompanied by the old woman whom the first daSilva had spoken of, and whom I too felt I knew in a mixed futuristic order of memory and event. It suddenly occurred to me that I was premature in thinking she had come of her free will. I suddenly saw—what I had known and dreaded from the very beginning—she was under arrest. Donne had made her come just short of the coarsest persuasion and apprehension he would exercise in the future, hoping to gain information from her about the whereabouts of the rest of the fearful frightened folk.

I shook my head a little, trying hard to free myself from this new obsession. Was it possible that one's memory and apprehension of a tragic event would strike one's spirit before the actual happening had been digested? Could a memory spring from nowhere into one's belly and experience? I knew that if I was dreaming I could pinch myself and wake.

But an undigested morsel of recollection erased all present waking sensation and evoked a future time, petrifying and painful, confused and unjust.

I shook my head violently, trying harder than ever to picture the deathless innocence and primitive expectation that had launched our inverse craft. Had we made a new problematical start—a pure and imaginary game, I told myself in despair—only to strip ourselves of all logical sequence and development and time? and to fasten vividly on our material life as if it were a passing fragment and fantasy while the curious nebulosity of ourselves stood stubborn and permanent? and as if every solid force and reason and distraction were the cruel stream that mirrored our everlastingness? I felt I was caught in a principle of never-ending anxiety and fear, and it was impossible to turn back.

I saw that Donne was ageing in the most remarkable misty way. It was something in the light under the trees I said to myself shaking my head. The day had grown sultry and darker than morning and a burst of congealed lightning hung suspended in the atmosphere, threatening to close the long drought and the dry season of the year.

Thirty or forty seasons and years had wrenched from him this violent belt of youth to shape a noose in the air. A shaft from the forest and the heaven of leaves aged him into looking the devil himself. The brownness of his skin looked excessive pallor. He stooped in unconscious subjection I knew to the treachery and oppression in the atmosphere and his eyes were sunken and impatient in rage, burning with the intensity of horror and ambition. His hands open and closed of their own will, casting to the ground everything save the feeling of themselves and of the identity they wished to establish in the roots of their mortal and earthly sensation. He was an apparition that stooped before me and yet clothed me with the very frightful nature of the jungle exercising its spell over me. I could no longer feel myself shaken: dumb with a morsel of terror.

He started suddenly addressing the company in the lurid storm but it was as if he spoke only to himself. The whole crew were blasted and rooted in the soil of Mariella like imprisoned dead trees. I alone lived and faced him. Words came as from a frightened spiritual medium and translation. Meaning was petrified and congealed and then flashing and clear upon his rigid face and brow hanging in his own ultimatum and light.

The storm passed as quickly as it had begun. Every man came to life again. Donne was free of the hate he had shown, I thought, and a smile had been restored to him ingenuous as youth. He drew me aside leaving the old Arawak woman encircled by the crew.

"Why you're looking haggard as hell," he said to me in solicitude. "Put on ten years overnight, old man," he spoke with a knowledgeable air beneath his apparent freshness and youth. "It's the trip all the way from the coast I suppose. How do you feel? Up to another strenuous exercise and excursion? Afraid I've been deserted by every labouring hand I had, and I've got to go on the trail to find them. Think you would relish coming?"

I shook my head quickly and affirmatively.

"Do you know"—he was in a better mood than I could ever remember—"there's something in what you've been telling me, old chap." He tapped me on the chest significantly, "You do see the situation sensibly and constructively. I grant I have been cruel and harsh . . ." he paused reflectively.

"Yes," I prompted him.

"I have treated the folk badly," he admitted. "But you do know what this nightmare burden of responsibility adds up to, don't you? how gruesome it can be? I do wish," he spoke musingly, "someone would lift it from my shoulders. Maybe who knows" —he was joking—"you can. Your faith and intuition may be better than mine. I am beginning to lose all my imagination save that sometimes I feel I'm involved in the most frightful material slavery. I hate myself sometimes, hate myself for being the most violent taskmaster—I drive myself with no hope of redemption whatsoever and I lash the folk. If they do murder me I've earned it I suppose, and I don't see sometimes how I can escape it unless a different person steps into my shoes and accepts my confounded shadow. Some weight and burden I confess frankly," he laughed as at an image—alien to himself—he was painting. "Still I suppose," he had grown thoughtful, "there's a ghost of a chance. . ."

"Ghost of a chance of what?" I demanded, swept away by his curious rhetoric.

"Changing my ways," he spoke mildly and indifferently. "Not being so beastly and involved in my own devil's schemes any more. Perhaps there's a ghost of a chance that I can find a different relationship with the folk, who knows? Nothing to lose anyway by trying. I suppose it's what I've always really wanted." He spoke absentmindedly now, stooping to the fire and helping himself to a plate of fish. "God," he said to himself, eating with sudden awareness and appetite, "I am damnably hungry,"—brooding a little as he ate, his face growing severe as of old, spoilt, hard, childish with an old obsession and desire. He tapped me on the chest turning ruthless and charming and smiling. "Of course I cannot afford to lean too far backwards (or is it forwards?) can I? Balance and perspective, eh, Boy? Look what's happening now. Nearly everybody just vamoosed, vanished. They're as thoughtless and irresponsible as hell. I was lucky to find even this old bitch"—he pointed to the old Arawak woman—"still hanging around. You can never trust these Bucks you know but she seems harmless enough. Isn't it a fantastic joke that I have to bargain with them and think of them at all?" He spoke bitterly and incredulously. "Who would believe that these devils have title to the savannahs and to the region? A stupid legacy—aboriginal business and all that nonsense: but there it is. I've managed so far to make a place for myself—spread out myself amply as it were—and in a couple of years I shall have firm prescriptive title myself. If," he spoke bitterly again, "these Indians start to kick up the world of a rumpus now it could be embarrassing and I may have to face costly litigation in the courts down there"— he pointed across the wrinkled map of the Arawak woman's face in the vague direction of the Atlantic Ocean as towards a scornful pool in heaven —"to hold my own, not to speak of forfeiting a cheap handsome source of labour. It's all so blasted silly and complicated. After all I've earned a right here as well. I'm as native as they, ain't I? A little better educated maybe whatever in hell that means. They call me sir and curse me when I'm not looking." He licked his lips and smiled. "The only way to survive of course is to wed oneself into the family. In fact I belong already." His brow wrinkled a little and he pointed to his dark racial skin. "As much as Schomburgh or Cameron or anybody." He could not help laughing, a sudden set laugh like a mask.

"We're all outside of the folk," I said musingly. "Nobody belongs yet. . . ."

"Is it a mystery of language and address?" Donne asked quickly and mockingly.

"Language, address?" I found it hard to comprehend what he meant. "There is one dreaming language I know of . . ." I rebuked him . . . "which is the same for every man. . . . No it's not language. It's . . . it's" . . . I searched for words with a sudden terrible rage at the difficulty I experienced . . . "it's an inapprehension of substance," I blurted out, "an actual fear . . . fear of life . . . fear of the substance of life, fear of the substance of the folk, a cannibal blind fear in oneself. Put it how you like," I cried, "it's fear of acknowledging the true substance of life. Yes, fear I tell you, the fear that breeds bitterness in our mouth, the haunting sense of fear that poisons us and hangs us and murders us. And somebody," I declared "must demonstrate the unity of being, and *show* . . ." I had grown violent and emphatic . . . "that fear is nothing but a dream and an appearance . . . even death . . ." I stopped abruptly.

Donne was not listening to my labour and expression and difficulty. He already knew by heart my unpredictable outbursts and attacks and inmost frenzy. Old Schomburgh and the Arawak woman stood at his side.

"What does she say?" he demanded. "You know the blasted Buck talk."

Old Schomburgh cleared his throat. He disciplined his voice to reply with the subservience of a shrewd labouring man. "They reach far away by now," he said awkwardly. "They moving quick and they know the trails."

"We must follow and overtake them," Donne said promptly.

"They accustom to move at this season, sir," Schomburgh spoke like a man making an obscure excuse. "Some kind of belief to do with the drought—once in seven year it bound to curse the land . . ." he paused and cleared his throat again.

"What's this to do with me Schomburgh?" Donne demanded.

"By Christmas when the hard time blow over they come back." Schomburgh spoke brokenly. "They gone to look for rain to plant easy-easy younder." He pointed. "By Christmas they come back." He stopped and I saw the light of uncertainty in his eye. "Perhaps we best to wait right here for them to come back, sir?" he pleaded.

"Are you mad, Schomburgh?" Donne cried. "Listen Uncle," it was his turn to plead and throw all stiffness to the winds, "find out—you know the Buck lingo—how we can catch up. I must have help in a month's time at latest, and that's long-long before you dream to see them back. Why the drought nearly done, and I got to have labour for my estate, my new rice planting, my cattle, everything. The folk just all can't bloody well run away. It's a hell of a superstitious unreasonableness. O Christ, don't look so sad man, ask her."

"She tell me already," Schomburgh cried awkwardly. "If we follow the river we going catch up in seven day time at a place where they bound to ford the water. . . ."

"Why in hell you didn't say so before?" Donne laughed and cried.

"Look, you going to you death," Schomburgh shouted and threatened suddenly. "To you death I say. I know. The river bad like a devil topside of this Mission. I know." It was an involuntary croaking outburst of which he grew instantly ashamed.

Jennings, the mechanic, wiped his hands nervously on his pants. "Is true, sir," he addressed Donne. "Is a dangerous time of the year to venture higher. Look what a bad time we had already."

"You fellows losing your fire or what?" Donne shot at him. "I thought this was a *crew* when we started."

"I vote to go," the daSilva twin exclaimed who had helped Cameron.

Jennings turned furious. "You potagee fool," he cried, "shut you mouth for a change. I is a young married man, two kiddy, and an old sick mother to mend. . . ." He was no longer wiping his hands on his pants but pointing a black angry finger in daSilva's face.

"I thought you knew all of that at the beginning," Donne shouted cold and sharp. "Look here, did you, or did you not, tell me you joined us because you were fed up—anything for a clean break? You wanted the water-top again you said. I pointed out how dangerous a season it was and you said you knew. You had had a narrow escape before, you had escaped by the skin of your teeth, you said. But it hadn't frightened you, you said. In fact when you felt you were dying you knew what a cowardly waste your life was. Anything was better you promised yourself than living again with a harridan and a shrew. Those were your words. Now tell me, Jennings do you wish us to stay right here and rot?" His voice had grown wretched and powerful. He knew he had to hold the crew to his side or he was lost.

"I know," Jennings said surlily. All of a sudden he grinned and began wiping his hands again on his grease-stained engineer's pants. "The truth is—you done know it already, so why pretend?—the folk I come from—me wife and me mother and me two child—believe I dead," he said. "Good for them and good for me. I like it right here under the trees. I vote to stop." He glared at the fateful propeller in the water as if that were the cause of all his trouble.

Cameron scowled at Jennings. "Shit," he said. "Let's move. we got to keep turning. I vote like daSilva to go." He adopted a belligerent air but he too, was heartily uncertain and afraid.

Carroll had begun laughing and the fresh ringing sound of his voice made everyone forget himself and turn in involuntary surprise. The laugh struck them as the slyest music coming clear out of the stream. It was like a bell and it startled away for one instant every imagined revolution of misery and fear and guile. It was an ingenuous sound like the homely crackle of gossiping parrots or of inspired branches in the leaves, or the slicing ecstasy and abandonment of the laughing wood when the hunter loses and finds his game in the footmark he has himself left and made.

Carroll laughed because he could not help himself. He saw that the omens and engines of grace and salvation were so easily turned again into doom. He felt—without clearly understanding why—that the entire crew had been drawn together almost against their will it seemed now and that their living desire was ambivalent and confused as the origin of the first command they dimly recalled and knew in the grave of memory. Something had freed them and lifted them up out of the deeps, a blessing and a curse, a reverberating clap of thunder and still music and song. The sound was jubilant and obscure and tremulous in their ear like a dreaming sword that had cut them from the womb.

Wishrop and Vigilance stood silent listening to the sound of the sword and the bell in the stream. Wishrop was a man of about forty, I dreamed, scanning his features with the deepest attention. A strong aquiline face it was, and still delicate and retiring in mood. I remember how he balanced himself and stood with the promise of a dancer on the prow of the boat when it moved in midstream. He spoke infrequently and as brokenly and whimsically as his labouring companions. His desire for communication was so profound it had broken itself into two parts. One part was a congealed question-mark of identity—around which a staccato inner dialogue and labouring monologue was in perpetual evolution and process. The other half was the fluid fascination that everyone and everything exercised upon him—creatures who moved in his consciousness full of the primitive feeling of love purged of all murderous hate and treachery.

He sought to excuse his deficiency and silence by declaring that he knew better Spanish than English. It was a convenient lie and it carried the ring of truth since he had lived for many years on the Guiana, Venezuela border. A look of unconscious regret and fear would flash when he spoke as if he feared he had already said too much. The crew knew what his guilt signified. He had whispered to them at various half-crazy times that he was dead for the record. He had told them secretly he would be a wanted man now, wanted for murder if it was known he was living. And so he wished to stay dead, he shouted, though he was perfectly alive.

He was mad they all knew. And yet harmless as a dove. They could not conceive of him as a real murderer. They preferred to accept his story as myth. He was an inspired vessel in whom they poured not only the longing for deathless obedience and constancy (which they read in his half-shadowed face) but the cutting desperate secret ambition he swore he had once nourished—the love that became its colder opposite—the desire they too felt, in their vicarious day-dream, to kill whatever they had learnt to hate. This dark wish was the deepest fantasy they knew mankind to entertain.

As deep as the nameless fish Schomburgh sometimes hooked whose flat beady eyes and skulls made him shiver and fling them back into the river. Electric eels for example. His hands twitched with shock in the presence of these playful absurd monsters as before a spirit of innocent malady and corruption he knew in his blood and bone. Old as the hills it was, this electrification and crucifixion of the mind.

Wishrop had dared to kill what he had learnt to hate. That was his mythical recommendation. He had dared to purge himself free—to execute what troubled him, to pluck from a phantom body both its arm and its eye of evil.

The boon companions with whom he lived at the extremity of the known world were thieves. And the women were whores. They slaved for gold and diamonds, the most precious thing they knew. Wishrop did not feel himself superior to anyone. He was honest because of a native inborn fastidiousness like a man who loved wiping and cleaning himself for no earthly reason. He never wanted to conceal diamonds in his mouth and lodge them between the toes of his feet after a day's work in the pits. Yet since everyone did it he accepted the principle and the practice. At that moment he started hating the phantom that was himself.

He saw himself reflected intimately in one of the women, dreamt he was in love with her, and unable to resist the challenge and the destiny of hate, married her and set her up to prove himself and his gods. The catechist who performed the ceremony sniggered behind his book. Wishrop marked him and never forgave him, swearing he was married now for good to the devil's country, and that he had started courting hell and disaster.

He came upon his wife in bed with another man, and suddenly swept by a cold hard virginal joy and pleasure, knew abruptly, here was what he had waited upon to begin; he shot the couple in the head through the eye. He repaired to the drinking saloon cold and mad in his pride. The boon companions were riddled, astonished and surprised, waving their hand vaguely to the blind bullet.

He shot the catechist stone-dead and sniggering under a couple of whores on the pathway leading to church. Lastly himself.

That was the end save that Wishrop woke to find himself still alive; and crawling out of the fracas into the bush he met the inevitable Arawak woman (this was the crew's ancestral embroidery and obsession) who nursed him to life. In the mortal hullaballoo that followed the muse reported that she had seen Wishrop crawling like a spider into the river where he had been tangled in the falls. Days after she pointed out his curious skeleton picked clean by perai, and that was the last of dead Wishrop.

The living Wishrop awoke overwhelmed by a final spasm of murderous fury and he shot the poor Arawak woman, his muse and benefactress. The curtain vanished upon this last act removing the web of death within himself. An eternity dawned.

His victims had never perished, constantly moving before him, living and never dying in the eternal folk.

His faith and optimism endeared him to the crew and they fed upon his brief confessions and ravings as the way of a vicarious fury and freedom and wishful action they had known, not believing a word in the improbable tale he told of a harmless lover and lunatic: nevertheless they pledged themselves anew to the sense of their indestructibility.

BOOK III

The Second Death

I tune the instrument here at the door,
And what I must do then, think here before.

JOHN DONNE

7

The crew came around like one man to the musing necessity in the journey beyond Mariella. We set out in the rising sun as soon as the mist had vanished. We had in our midst a new member sitting crumpled-looking, like a curious ball, old and wrinkled. Her long black hair—with the faintest glimmer of silvery grey—hung in two plaits down to her waist. She sat still as a bowing statue, the stillness and surrender of the American Indian of Guiana in reflective pose. Her small eyes winked and blinked a little. It was an emotionless face. The stiff brooding materiality and expression of youth had vanished, and now—in old age—there remained no sign of former feeling. There was almost an air of crumpled pointlessness in her expression, the air of wisdom that a millennium was past, a long timeless journey was finished without appearing to have begun, and no show of malice, enmity and overt desire to overcome oppression and evil mattered any longer. She belonged to a race that neither forgave nor forgot. That was legend. In reality the legend and consciousness of race had come to mean for her—patience, the unfathomable patience of a god in whom all is changed into wisdom, all experience and all life a handkerchief of wisdom when the grandiloquence of history and civilization was past. It was the subtlest labour and sweat of all time in the still music of the senses and of design.

Her race was a vanishing one overpowered by the fantasy of a Catholic as well as a Protestant invasion. This cross she had forgiven and forgotten in an earlier dream of distant centuries and a returning to the Siberian unconscious pilgrimage in the straits where life had possessed and abandoned at the same time the apprehension of a facile beginning and ending. An unearthly pointlessness was her true manner, an all-inclusive manner that still contrived to be—as a duck sheds water from its wings—the negation of every threat of conquest and of fear—every shade of persecution wherein was drawn and mingled the pursued and the pursuer alike, separate and yet one and the same person. It was a vanishing and yet a starting race in which long eternal malice and wrinkled self-defence and the cruel pursuit of the folk were turning into universal protection and intuition and that harmonious rounded miracle of spirit which the world of appearances had never truly known.

Before the sun was much higher we were in the

grip of the straits of memory. The sudden dreaming fury of the stream was naught else but the ancient spit of all flying insolence in the voiceless and terrible humility of the folk. Tiny embroideries resembling the handwork on the Arawak woman's kerchief and the wrinkles on her brow turned to incredible and fast soundless breakers of foam. Her crumpled bosom and river grew agitated with desire, bottling and shaking every fear and inhibition and outcry. The ruffles in the water were her dress rolling and rising to embrace the crew. This sudden insolence of soul rose and caught them from the powder of her eyes and the age of her smile and the dust in her hair all flowing back upon them with silent streaming majesty and abnormal youth and in a wave of freedom and strength.

The crew were transformed by the awesome spectacle of a voiceless soundless motion, the purest appearance of vision in the chaos of emotional sense. Earthquake and volcanic water appeared to seize them and stop their ears dashing the scales only from their eyes. They saw the naked unequivocal flowing peril and beauty and soul of the pursuer and the pursued all together, and they knew they would perish if they dreamed to turn back.

"Is War Office," Schomburgh screamed but his voice was silent and dead in his throat. And then the full gravity and climax of our predicament came home to us. We had entered the War Office rapids, a forbidden passage, deceived by the symbols in the inhuman drought of the year, and by the bowing submissive rock that guarded the river. We should have kept to the other bank in this season of nature. To turn back now and ride the stream was to be swept so swiftly and unpredictably along we were bound to crash and collide and collapse. The only course was to fight, glued to the struggle, keeping our bow silent and straight in the heart of an unforgiving and unforgivable incestuous love. This fantasy had descended upon us like a cloud out of the sun. Everyone blamed everyone else for being the Jonah and for having had an evil intercourse with fate. Donne had arrested the witch of a woman and we had aided and abetted him. A murderous rape and fury filled our heart to an overburden, it seemed, nevertheless balanced and held in check by our voiceless impossible wrestle and struggle in the silent passage in the lava of water. We were screwed to boat and paddle in sending the vessel forward inch by inch. The spinning propeller spun in Jennings's head and beneath our graven feet. The great cloud sealed our eyes again and we saw only the spirit that had raped the old woman and invoked upon us our own answering doom in her daemonic-flowing presence and youth. We began to gripe and pray interminably and soundlessly.

Carroll—the youngest in the crew—stood up quickly as though he had been inspired to behold Schomburgh's straining difficulty at the bow and Wishrop's helpless engagement with Donne at the stern. He had hardly made a step when he appeared to slip and to fall with a cry into the water. He disappeared silently and completely. The crew set up a further cry which was as helpless as a dream. The old woman bent over the water, suddenly rolling a little in her seat. She looked old as ever, old as she had looked fantastically young and desirable before. The crew were filled with the brightest-seeming clarity of tragedy, as cloudless as imperfectly true as their self-surrender to the hardship of the folk they followed and pursued: the cloudy scale of incestuous cruelty and self-oppression tumbled from their eye leaving only a sense of disconsolate flying compassion and longing. Their ears were unstopped at last and they heard plainly Vigilance's pointing cry as well as their own shout penetrating their ears with the grief and the musical love and value in the stricken fall and sacrifice of youth. In an instant it were as if we saw with our own eyes as well as heard with our own ears an indestructible harmony within the tragedy and the sorrow of age and the malice and the nature of youth. It was Carroll's voice and head that turned to stone and song, and the sadness of the baptismal lamentation on his lips which we heard in the heart of the berserk waters was our own almost senseless rendering and apprehension of the truth of our art and our perfection in the muse.

The boat seemed to gain momentum as though every effort we made carried a new relationship within it. The water heaped itself into a musing ball upon which we rolled forward over and beyond the rapids. The stream grew wide and gentle as a sheet, and with a sigh we relinquished our paddles—save at stern and bow—and allowed ourselves to be propelled forward by Jennings's engine.

I knew that a great stone of hardship had melted and rolled away. The trees on the bank were clothed in an eternity of autumnal colour—equally removed from the green of youth as from the iron-clad winter of age—a new and enduring spiritual summer of russet and tropical gold whose tints had been tenderly planted in the bed of the stream. The sun veined these mythical shades and leaves in our eye. Old Schomburgh had been relieved by Vigilance and he sat silent and wondering and staring in the water. No one had dared broach Carroll's name out of some strange inner desire not to lose the private image and thought within us which at the moment bore our gratitude and our mature joy and sadness more deeply than seasonal words.

Carroll was one of the old man's beloved nephews.

Schomburgh knew him first as a lad arriving from a distant mission, a little inquisitorial, but much more shy and wistful than dogmatic he had appeared after dawdling his time away in idleness and speculation far from Sorrow Hill where Schomburgh lived. He was seventeen, and a shocking long time it was, Schomburgh said, he had been idle. Now at last he had deigned to think of looking for a real job on the watertop (when he had already wasted so much time) Schomburgh scolded his nephew. He remembered it all now with a shock as he sat staring from the bow of the boat—the intimate cold shock of old that had served to bait the guilt he had already felt and known even before his new nephew came. There had always been a thorn in acknowledging his relationships—an unexplored cloud of promiscuous wild oats he secretly dreaded. His family tree subsisted in a soil of entanglement he knew to his grief in the stream of his secretive life, and Carroll's arrival brought the whole past to a head before him. Still Carroll proved himself in the fits and starts of the older man's dreaming adventures to be superior to the ambivalent ominous creature he first looked to be. He was tough, tougher than expectation. He slept easy as an infant on the hardest ground. His bones were those of a riverman, hard and yet fluid in emergency, and his senses grew attuned to musical footmarks and spiritual game.

Many an evening he borrowed Cameron's guitar and his painstaking light-hearted predisposition to melody emerged and touched the listening harp in every member of the crew. No one knew where or what it was. Schomburgh felt the touch of harmony without confessing a response when in the midst of his evening recreation with rod and line in the stream he listened deeply to the stirrings within himself. He would suddenly catch himself and declare he had found the hoax that was being played upon him.

And still he knew it was impossible to abandon an inexplicable desire and hope, the invisible pull in his fingers, a tautness and tension within, around which had been wrapped all doubtful matter and flesh like bait on a fisherman's hook. A long bar of secret music would pass upon the imbedded strings and his flesh quaked and shook. The nervous tension of the day—that had now rooted him in the bow—had broken every barrier of memory and the tide came flooding upon him. He felt the fine stringed bars of a universal ecstasy tuning within him beyond life and death, past and present, until they neither ceased nor stopped.

He was a young man again—in the prime of maturity—meeting his first true invisible love. She had appeared out of the forest—from a distant mission—far from Sorrow Hill. She was as dark as the curious bark of a tree he remembered, and round and promising like sapodilla. Schomburgh was a stranger to her it seemed (she had not yet discovered his name) fair-skinned, older by wiser years, athletic and conscious in his half-stooping, half-upright carriage of an ancient lineage and active tradition amongst the riverfolk.

What a chase it was. He cornered her and poured upon her his first and last outburst of frenzied self-forgetting eloquence until he felt the answer of her lips. She smelt like leaves growing on top the rocks in the sun in the river, a dry and yet soft bursting smell, the dryness of the hot scampering sun on the fresh inwardness of a strong resilient plant. She smelt dry and still soft. The vaguest kerchief of breath had wiped her brow after her exertion running with fear and joy.

He had hardly found her when she had gone. So incredible it was he rubbed his eyes again as he sat staring into the water. He set out after her but it was as if a superior fury—insensible and therefore stronger and abler than he—had propelled her away. It dawned upon him—like an inward tremor and voice—that she had learnt his name—from what source and person he did not know since she had spent such a very short time at Sorrow Hill—and this had engineered her suspicion and flight. Dread seized his mind, the dread of sexual witchcraft. He drew at last to the distant door of the Mission where she lived, and the dubious light of the fantastic wheel of dawn strengthened and sliced his mind. It was an ancient runaway home of his father's he had reached. His father had settled here late in life—with a new mistress—and founded a separate family. Some said he guillotined his birthright for a song, a flimsy strip of a thing, beautiful as a fairy. All was rumour and legend without foundation. Even as a boy Schomburgh had known the truth and dismissed the exaggerated fairy-tale. His father was dead. That was the living truth. And yet he could not stir one step beyond where he now stood. He stood there it seemed for the passage of months until he grew greyer than the ghost of the stars and the moon and the sun. She was waiting for him he told himself, like any young girl—frightened in a first indiscretion and affair—nevertheless waiting for love to enter and take her everlastingly. Her folk and parents would kill the fatted calf and welcome him like a son. He shuddered, and the vibration struck him inwardly, a lamentation in the wind, fingers on the strings of his spirit, the melancholy distant sound of a raining harp. His fear and horror lifted a little as he heard it—riveted to the ghostly threshold and ground of his life. It no longer mattered whether Carroll was his nephew or his son or both. He had heard clearer than ever before the distant music of the heart's wish and desire. But even now he tried to resist and rebuke himself for being merely another nasty sentimental old man.

Vigilance bowed for Schomburgh, his paddle glancing and whirling along the gunwhale, equally alert and swift on both sides when the occasion demanded. His penetrating trained eye saw every rock, clothing it with a lifelikeness that mirrored all past danger and design. His vision of peril meant an instantaneous relationship to safety. He offered himself to the entire crew—as he bowed—a lookout to prove their constant reality—and he hid his tears from everyone. The truth was Carroll was his stepbrother. Vigilance had introduced him to Uncle Schomburgh, and the old man had stared at the ultimate ghost he both dreaded and loved.

Vigilance had been a boy of thirteen when his father had taken Carroll's mother into his house as his wife, the boy Carroll, her only child, being four or five years old then. Vigilance was the eldest of seven, and their mother had died a couple of months ago in her last childbirth. Carroll's mother thus became the adopted mother of the Vigilance brood who were lucky to get such a young woman and stepmother for the large family, the youngest of whom was an infant two months old.

She was lucky too to find the protection of the Vigilance family for her child whose father no one had ever seen. The name the child bore was little-known in those parts. Her husband bore her no malice and wished her son to take his name as a final safeguard. This she resisted. She felt it would do no good—the name Carroll was as innocuous and distant a name as any she could choose. She did not wish to attract upon her head and the head of her new family the hoax of sin in an implacable future. Vigilance could not remember ever addressing his stepbrother as anything else but Carroll. In fact this habit of using the surname was the curious custom amongst most families in the enormous dreaming forest who dreaded mislaying and losing each other. After a time everybody believed Carroll's name was a true one. It were as if they had a long and a short memory at one and the same time so that while they forgot the name Carroll's mother had borne (as one is inclined to forget maiden names) they helped to invent and forge a name for her son which established distant ties they only dimly dreamt of. Carroll was one burning memory and substance for his mother and another dimmer incestuous substance and myth for his uncertain and unknown father folk. He had become a relative ghost for all as all ultimately became a ghost for everyone.

It was a strange and confusing tradition beyond

words. Vigilance saw that Schomburgh had been overwhelmed in some unnatural way that fractured his vision and burdened him with a sense of fantasy and hoax. It was the darkest narcissism that strove with him and fought against accepting Carroll's name as Carroll, against relinquishing paternity to some one who was still untouched by and unknown to the spirit of guilt. He wished to give the boy his own name but the desire frightened and killed him. No one knew and understood better than a mother what a name involved. It was the music of her undying sacrifice to make and save the world. Sometimes he accepted and grew enamoured of the thought that Carroll was his nephew and nothing else. Often times he lived in the flight of mortal gloom and fear Carroll was nothing to him at all, a bastard memory from a bastard hellish tribe and succession and encounter. Who and what was Carroll? Schomburgh had glimpsed, Vigilance knew with an inborn genius and primitive eye, the living and the dead folk, the embodiment of hate and love, the ambiguity of everyone and no-one. He had recognized his true son, nameless out of shame and yet named with a new distant name by a muse and mother to make others equally nameless out of mythical shame and a name, and to forge for their descendants new mythical farflung relationships out of their nameless shame and fear.

Vigilance read this material hoax and saw deeper

than Schomburgh to the indestructible element. It was a simple lesson for him since he was born to discern and reflect everything without the conscious effort of speech.

His eyes were brighter than ever after their fit of crying. The past returned to him like pure fictions of rock he had never wearied spying upon since childhood. Sometimes they stood in columns, or they embraced each other in groups, or in couples, or they stood solitary and alone.

Donne was the only one in their midst who carried on his sleeve the affectation of a rich first name. Rich it seemed—because none of his servants appeared at first to have the power to address him other than obsequiously. The manner of the crew could change, however, one sensed, into familiarity and contempt. It was on their lips already to declare that their labouring distress and dream was the sole tradition of living men.

He had come from a town on the coast they knew to found and settle, be baptized again, as well as to baptize, a new colony. He was careless of first name and title alike they saw. All were economic names to command and choose from (as one chose to order one's labouring folk around). All were signs of address from a past dead investment and history with its vague pioneering memories that were more their burden than his.

They knew he had once dreamt of ruling them with a rod of iron and with a ration of rum. His design was so brutal and clear that one wondered how one could be so cheap to work for him. There was nothing he appeared to have that commended him. Save the nameless kinship of spirit older (though he did not yet apprehend it) than every material mask and label and economic form and solipsism. Vigilance had seen clear into the bowels of this nameless kinship and identity Donne had once thought he had abused as he wished, and in one stroke it had liberated him from death and adversity.

He recalled as he bowed that his father had built a new house after the second marriage. The three-roomed cabin—his first home—remained; a stone's throw away stood the new rough-hewn spacious five-roomed cottage into which the family had moved.

It was natural to Vigilance to perceive what was going on wherever he lived. He was always *there* when his parents spoke, or he always seemed to *see* something through a half-open door or window or crack. It was a habit of fortune he possessed, ingrained and accidental as all remarkable coincidences are.

The new house was a year old, and his father was away that afternoon for a couple of days on a wood-cutting mission. The rest of the family were busy far afield outdoors.

Carroll and his mother had just come in. He saw them in the next room through an open door. They were so flustered-looking and inwardly disturbed that they had no eyes for him.

"She lose the baby, she lose me baby, she lose she baby," Carroll was crying to his mother, all his shyness and charm fractured and gone. Vigilance knew instantly they were speaking of his sister; she happened to be a couple of years younger than Carroll who had just attained his seventeenth birthday.

"O love," Carroll's mother cried to him. "Is lucky", she nearly bit her lips, broken in their emotion. "No, no, not lucky. I wrong. But I mean is just as well. Think what your stepfather would say." She wrung her hands.

"I can marry her. She's not my blood-sister," Carroll spoke glumly and half-dementedly.

"No, no," his mother cried. "She too young to marry. I going take care of her." She smoothed Carroll's unhappy brow. He jerked away a little. "Why, why?" he cried. "Why?"

"You got to travel and see the world," his mother said sadly, looking at him as if she dared not touch him again. "You don't know what is a wife feeling yet. You don't know anything. You got to make your fortune. Look," she wrung her hands again, "from the day you born to me I see you were different. You were a problem. I feel as if you was not even me child. A strange funny child in me hands. As if you didn't belong to me at all, at all. If you stay here is only trouble going come under this roof. And you stepfather is a good kind man I love," she suddenly grew quiet and spoke softly. Then she cried—"Mek yourself into a man and *then* come back. Is a different story then."

Carroll's eyes flashed and he moved further away from her still—"I is not as soft as I look. I can live and work hard. I can mek me way to the ends of the earth. I born to go far." He was boasting and still sad. "Like you don't know me at all."

His mother was sadder still. "Is best you go," she said. Her lips were torn and they looked burnt with the sun.

"I don't want to leave she," Carroll cried. "I can tek she with me and tek care of she and she tek care of me." He cried to her louder than ever.

"Your stepfather would forbid it," his mother said passionately.

"I can carry she and look after she," Carroll said sullenly.

"You think life so simple?" his mother pleaded with him. "You got to earn you fortune, lad. Sometimes is the saddest labour in the world."

"You mean if I mek a million dollar and come back I can claim she as me wife?" Carroll said.

"If you mek a million dollar you think you can

fool the living and bring the dead alive?" His mother spoke strangely. "Is not money make me flesh and fortune."

"I can mek it all up to she. She suffer bad-bad. She had a fall. We did plan to run and marry soon as she start to show big. She was a child yet." His voice broke.

"Everything going be all right," his mother tried to soothe him. "Everything going be right as rain. Right as a song. Make you fortune and come back." She spoke sadly as if she knew his fortune was the despair of mere flesh and blood.

"We been playing a year ago," Carroll said musingly. "Suddenly we lose we way in the trees. We think we never find home. We started hugging, a frighten sweet-sweet feeling like if I truly come home. I wasn't a stranger no more. She cry a little and she laugh like if she was home at last. And she kiss me after it all happen. . . ."

"How you know she was with baby?" his mother asked after a long silence.

"One day I hear a heart, clear-clear . . . I wanted to tell somebody. But I was afraid even to tell you. Until today when she fall and she cry in she pain I was so afraid . . ." he cried and his voice sounded like hers. "Did you hear anything?" he said a little wildly, looking out of the window. "Was a terrible fall. You hear anything?"

"Impossible," his mother rebuked him. "You couldn't have heard that infant heart beating so small and long ago. . . Three or four months ago. . . ."

"I hear it," Carroll insisted and his voice fell and broke into two again.

His mother smiled as if she had forgotten him. "Maybe is true," she said, "I hear it too." She rubbed herself gently on her belly.

"You," Carroll shot at her.

"Yes," she caught herself. His eyes probed hers deep. She spoke like one seeking forgiveness. "I am with child for your stepfather too," she expressed herself awkwardly. Her voice broke into two like his. "My first child under his roof after so long and I getting old. . ."

Carroll nodded his head dumbly. "Is the child as old as. . . ?" he choked with alarm and fear.

"Yes," she nodded.

"A boy or a girl?" he asked foolishly.

"Was a boy," she said. "I saw." They were at cross purposes. "If you go and come back you will find the child," she sighed.

"His child borning and mine dead," he spoke passionately, forgetting to whom he spoke.

"No," his mother said sharply. "Is all one in the long run. You can make peace between us. . . ."

"And go?" he demanded. He was crying. Suddenly

he knew he did not want the child in her to live. A heart-rending spasm overwhelmed him, all ancestral hate and fear and jealousy.

"You are my child always," his mother spoke softly. Her lips twisted again. "You must live and go. Is your own will if you stay to rot and die since you will start to imagine foolish things. Go I tell you." She spoke softly again.

Carroll ran out of the house blindly toward the cabin in the woods where Tiny, the Vigilance sister, lay. She looked old and sad lying there he thought, wrinkled in his imagination. He saw her as an old woman in the future, wrinkled and wise, the memory of her mythical incestuous child come again—living and strong as life. It was as if he came to his spiritual mother at last, and the effect of his child's death had sealed and saved the maternal pregnancy and womb beyond all jealousy and fear and doubt.

Carroll's mother looked up suddenly with a sense of unexplored and inexplicable joy. She was startled when she saw Vigilance. "You here?" she cried. "How long you been listening?"

Vigilance nodded dumbly. He did not know what to say. He knew that the child she carried for his father would live, and bear the eyes of the living and the dead. He felt drawn towards it as towards a child of his own.

"You are free to go too, and this time take him with you for ever when you go," his stepmother addressed him with a curious blessing smile.

8

We stood on the frontiers of the known world, and on the self-same threshold of the unknown.

Schomburgh was dead. He had died peacefully in his hammock and in his sleep.

The old crumpled Arawak woman had advised us the evening of the day before where to stop and camp for the night. It was too late she said (Schomburgh interpreting) to venture into the nameless rapids that seethed and boiled before us.

We buried Schomburgh at the foot of the broken water whose agitation was witness of the forces that lay ahead.

Carroll was dead. Schomburgh was dead. One death, a cross for father and son. They had been ghosts to each other in the limited way a man grasped reality. Schomburgh often inhabited Carroll's shoes running from and toward his love the day it was born and had died. Carroll often listened, almost worshipping the hoax of death and age and sin in Schomburgh's boots, like a child prematurely stricken and old with the passage of mortal conception and thought. It had been an enormous endless growing pain and fantasy—rich with the wealth of unexplored possibilities—all over and done with and secure. They had sown and won a great liberal fortune for the whole world though the full fruitage and inheritance lay yet in the future and time.

Everyone paid silent tribute in the breakfastless empty morning. None dared to say anything yet knowing their common speech was the debased coinage and currency of the dreaming folk. Silence seemed golden now and superior to the universal mask and ironic disavowal of principle in the nameless indestructible soul. The broken speech of the crew died awhile on their lips though in their affections they still heard themselves speak in the old manner of distortion and debasement. It was the inevitable and unconscious universe of art and life that still harassed and troubled them.

DaSilva broke the golden silence and expressed his misgivings aloud. "Is how much further we got to go?" He spoke to himself, forgetting his destination and turning helplessly to the old Arawak woman. There was no interpreter now Schomburgh had gone. A wrench had uprooted the instrument of communication he had always trusted in himself. And yet he knew it was a mortal relief to face the truth which lay farther and deeper than he dreamed. This deathblow of enlightenment robbed him of a facile faith and of a simple translation and memory almost.

"Is how much farther we got to go?" he cried in his helpless dull way. "The Buck woman can't speak a word."

Donne started unrolling his plan quickly. The country ahead was mysterious and little known he said. A long series of dangerous rapids marked the map in his hands. The neighbouring country was mountainous and crude, the trails secret and hidden. One day had passed since they left Mariella. And today—the second of the allotted seven before them—had started with an omen of good fortune, strange and shattering as it seemed. They were on the threshold of the folk. They must cling to that knowledge since—he had never seen it so clear before—it was all they had.

He felt the clearest keenest perception of their need and security. Remember—he said—when they entered the world ahead—the world of the second day—they had passed the door of inner perception like a bird of spirit breaking the shell of the sky which had been the only conscious world all knew. In the death of their comrades, the cross of father-and-son, Donne said pedantically and sorrowfully, they had started on the way to overcoming a sacred convention of evil proprietorship and gain.

The crew drew around as he turned to practical

issues in hand. "Today we will reach *here*," he pointed to a little indentation where he proposed to camp next. "Tomorrow . . ." his voice droned on and on.

"One shear pin snap in that water and all gone," Jennings sang out. He was frowning. He pushed his way until he stood face to face with Donne. "All this is a lot of balls," he said.

"You can stay here if you wish," Donne said calmly. "I will drive the motor, Vigilance will bow and Wishrop—on whom I feel I can lean more than ever—will steer. The three of us alone will go if need be, come what may. And as a matter-of-fact the daSilvas and Cameron are still with us I believe? We can do with their help." He turned to the crew. They nodded a little.

Jennings was partly taken aback. "O, you want to leave me here, you do?" he shouted.

"Matter entirely for you," said Donne.

Jennings laughed. Fine lines of sweat—customary to him—stood out again. His laugh resounded like a trumpet. Clearly—it came like a revelation—whatever the beads on his brow—he was without fear. A stubborn nameless streak rose and sweated him into a man who wanted a fight. Irritation and resentment boiled within him against all authority and responsibility. He saw too clearly and harshly the strength of his mechanical arm and position and the farce and guile and deception he had always experienced. The knowledge burned him and invigorated him at the same time with the honey of justification and leisure and laziness in palate and nostril. He was as good as any man he knew. "You can't fool me no more," he said. "All of you *bastards*—high and mighty alike. If I come with all you is of me own sweet will. You can't *fool* me no more." His voice brayed like a resurrection trumpet over the dead.

"Who want to fool you" said Cameron. His heart was suddenly beating fast and loud. A shaft of nameless misery had entered and wounded him. He had never felt this sensation before. Jennings loomed upon him now with a terrifying jeer and gibe on his lips.

"Who want to fool you?" Cameron cried again. He listened closely to his own voice. It was the voice of dread: the voice of dread at the thought that nothing existed to fool and terrorize anybody unless one chose to imagine one was bewitched and a fool all one's life. The terrible sound and vision struck him a blow, sharp and keen and intimate as a knife bursting into a drum. The ground felt that it opened bringing to ruin years of his pride and conceit.

"Who want to fool *you*?" Cameron shouted in rage and indignation. He wished desperately the oracular grave under his feet would close for ever and disappear and he could cherish once again his old pagan desire and ambition. It struck him like an acute dismemberment and loss and injustice.

Jennings jeered—"You silly dope, Cameron you," he laughed. "I shit on devils like you. By the time you fall out of one scrape you land in another. Who is you to ask me a thing?"

"What I want to know—" Cameron was in a greater rage than ever "who trying to fool who?"

"O buzz off"—Jennings laughed. "You is just anybody's plaything and wood, Cameron, a piece of what I call flotsam and jetsam"—he spoke jeeringly and a little sententiously, advertising his phrases and words. "Me?" he cried. "I is me own f—— revolution, equal to all, understand? I can stand pon the rotten ground face to face with the devil. And I don't gamble pon any witch in heaven or hell. I lef' that behind me long long ago." His voice grew wicked and chiding—"You is one of them old time labouring parasite, Cammy boy, you is such a big grown man but you still hankering for a witch and a devil like a child in a fairy-tale Cammy, boy. You must be learning more sense than that by now! You mean to say you ain't seeing daylight yet Cammy, me boy?"

Cameron saw red. His arm shot out and burst Jennings's mouth. Jennings's look lost its jeering ease and smile in a startled flash of surprise. He wiped his mouth, even as he tasted the salt on his lips, and he spied the blood on his hand. He sprang. Cameron took the over-eager blow on his shoulder, ducking where another deadly wild fist crashed to his skull. Jennings went mad and Cameron felt an onslaught such as he had never dreamed to face in his life. He defended himself, retaliating with the swiftest flying fists in the world. An overpowering sense of injury smote the air again and again in their joint nameless breath.

"Stop," Donne shouted. "Stop." The voice was so terrible and full of suppressed turbulence and demonic authority, it halted them like an overflow of scalding self-confidence and self-knowledge.

"Stop."

They were turned to stone stung to the bitterest attention by what they knew not. Jennings remained powerful, thrusting, the air of a primitive republican boxer upon him, and Cameron stood, heavy and bundled like rock, animal-wise, conscious of a rootless superstition and shifting mastery he had once worshipped in himself and now felt crumbling and lost. Donne stood pointing at them with an air of aristocratic fury beyond words. His eyes were liquid and misty and dark. It was a picture to be long remembered in an age that stood at the door of freedom though no one knew yet what that truly meant. It was a grave of idols and the resurrection of an incalculable devouring principle.

Once again the crew came around to the musing necessity in the second day's journey into the nameless rapids above Mariella. They had hardly entered the falls when they knew their lives were finished in the raging torrent and struggle. The shock of the nameless command and the breath of the water banished thought and the pride of mockery and convention as it banished every eccentric spar and creed and wishful certainty they had always adored in every past adventure and world.

They felt naked and helpless, unashamed of their nakedness and still ashamed in a way that was a new experience for them. They saw and heard only the boiling stream and furnace of an endless life without beginning and end. And the terror of this naked self-governing reality made them feel unreal and unwanted for ever in dreaming themselves up alive. They wished the man who stood before them, or next to them, was real and true and capable of exercising the last power of banishment over them by dismissing their own fiction and unreality and life.

The monstrous thought came to them that they had been shattered and were reflected again in each other at the bottom of the stream.

The unceasing reflection of themselves in each other made them see themselves everywhere save where they thought they had always stood.

After awhile this horrifying exchange of soul and this identification of themselves with each other brought them a partial return and renewal of confidence, a neighbourly wishful fulfilment and a basking in each other's degradation and misery that they had always loved and respected. It was a partial rehabilitation of themselves, the partial rehabilitation of a tradition of empty names and dead letters, dead as the buttons on their shirt. It was all well and good they reasoned as inspired madmen would to strain themselves to gain that elastic frontier where a spirit might rise from the dead and rule the material past world. All well and good was this resurgence and reconnoitre they reasoned. But it was doomed again from the start to meet endless catastrophe: even the ghost one dreams of and restores must be embalmed and featured in the old lineaments of empty and meaningless desire.

A groan rose from their lips to silence their half-hopeful half-treacherous thoughts that oscillated over their predicament as the sky dreams indifferently over the earth. The vessel had struck a rock. And they saw it was the bizarre rock and vessel of their second death. The life they had clung to and known before was turning into a backward incoherent dream of the first insensible death they had experienced. Even so a groan rose to their lips and a longing to re-establish that first empty living hollowness and brutal habitation. Surely ignorance was better than their present unendurable self-knowledge and discomfort. Their lips however were smothered and silenced in the hunger of spray.

The boat struck and glanced into the foaming current on the edge of overturning. Wishrop danced at the bow. His paddle hooked and caught a sharp point an inch beneath the belly of the vessel's wood. He hurtled into the air like a man riding a wheel. A nameless gasp riddled and splintered the crew. He vanished.

The boat appeared to right itself miraculously. And Jennings's machine—which Cameron kept a sturdy hand upon when Jennings had sprained his wrist in the struggle—sent a hideous strangled roar out of the water. It had lost its vulgar mechanical fervour and its enthusiasm was dwindling into an indefatigable revolving spider, hopeless and persistent.

Hopeless to dream of finding Wishrop in the maelstrom. He too had dwindled in a moment. They had seen his hands aloft two times quickly after his immersion for all the world like fingers clinging to the spokes and spider of a wheel. The webbed fingers caught and held for an instant a half-submerged rock but the crouching face was too slippery and smooth and they had slipped and gone. The wheeling water lifted him spread-eagled once again for an instant. He disappeared from their view. But rose still again—a skull on whom the hair had been plastered for a changeling demon. It was impossible to say. Anything was everything in the whirling swift moment and in the fantasy of their shattered boat and life. All rose and were submerged a hundred feet or yards apart or ages.

The boat still crawled, driven by the naked spider of spirit. Wishrop's flesh had been picked clean by perai like a cocerite seed in everyone's mouth. They shuddered and spat their own—and his—blood and death-wish. It had been forcibly and rudely ejected. And this taste and forfeiture of self-annihilation bore them into the future on the wheel of life.

The water moved past with reflective backward strokes as the vessel went forward. The old Arawak woman stirred a little, a sudden wind fluttering her sleeves. She had been sleeping all the while but now that the danger was past she had awakened. The river was familiar ground to her, it was plain. High precipitous cliffs and walls had appeared on either hand and bank. She blinked a little, pointing her aged and active fingers. Vigilance saw trees growing out of the cliffs overhead parallel to the river and he wondered whether any man could climb and clamber there. He rubbed his eyes since he felt he saw what no human mind should see, a spidery skeleton crawling to the sky. It danced and gambolled a little, clutching the vertical floor that seemed to change in a shaft of cloudy sun into a protean stream of coincidence where every mechanical revolution and image was the inscrutable irony of a spiritual fate.

Vigilance could not make up his bemused mind whether it was Wishrop climbing there or another version of Jennings's engine in the stream. He shrank from the image of his hallucination that was more radical and disruptive of all material conviction than anything he had ever dreamt to see. The precipitous cliffs were of volcanic myth and substance he dreamed far older than the river's bed and stream. He seemed to sense and experience its congealment and its ancient flow as if he waded with webbed and impossible half-spidery feet in the ceaseless boiling current of creation. His immateriality and mysterious substantiality made him dance and tremble with fear a little as Wishrop danced. It was incredible that one had survived. He saw into the depths of the deathless stream where the Arawak woman pointed. A flock of ducks flew, their wings pointed like stars. They were skeletons fixed from ancient geological time unmoving as a plateau.

The sudden whirr of their wings awoke him as they flew living and wild across the river. The Arawak woman laughed. Vigilance drew himself up like a spider in a tree. He stood over an archway and gate in the rock through which swarmed and streamed a herd of tapirs, creatures half-donkey and half-cow. They were seething with fear as they ploughed into the river.

"Look—chased by the folk," Donne said. He spoke from the bow of a skeleton craft Vigilance discerned in the stream of the rock. "Look one has been wounded and is dying. We are close as hell to the huntsman of the folk." His deathless image and look made the Arawak woman smile. Vigilance winced a little and rubbed his eyes where he climbed and clung to the cliff wondering at the childish repetitive boat and prison of life. What an enormous spiritual distance and inner bleeding substance lay between himself and that crust and shell he had once thought he inhabited. He could hardly believe it. He tried to convey across the span and gulf of dead and dying ages and myth the endless pursuit on which Donne was engaged.

"Rubbish," Donne said. "That herd is a good sign. The folk are not so far away. We can catch up and repair our fortunes. They'll lead us home safely and we'll cultivate our fields and our wives." He spoke out of a desire to hearten himself and the crew. The truth was he no longer felt himself in the land of the living though the traumatic spider of the sun crawled up and down his arms and his neck and punctured his sides of rock.

Vigilance was sensible to the fantasy of his wound and alive, the sole responsible survivor save for the Arawak woman who clung with him to the wall of rock. He dreamed she had kept her promise, her stepmotherly promise, and had saved him from drowning. Donne's boat had righted itself, he dreamed, in the volcanic stream and rock and the crew were all there save Wishrop's spider and transubstantiation: wheel and web, sunlight, starlight, all wishful substance violating and altering and annihilating shape and matter and invoking eternity only and space and musical filament and design. It was this spider and wheel of baptism—infinite and expanding—on which he found himself pinned and bent to the revolutions of life—that made his perception of a prodigal vessel and distance still possible. Darkness fell and the banks were too steep for the crew to land. The river had grown smooth and this was a great good fortune. The stream sang darkly and the stars and harmony of space turned into images of light.

The sun rose on the third day of their setting out from Mariella. The cliffs appeared to rise higher still on both hands and the river seemed to stretch endlessly and for ever onward. The water was as smooth as a child's mirror and newborn countenance.

Nevertheless the crew were downcast and dejected. They had forgotten the miraculous escape they had had and recalled only fear and anxiety and horror and peril. This was hard-hearted nature they contemplated without thinking they may have already overcome it and tamed it and escaped it. Rather it seemed to them only too clear that the past would always catch up with them—when they least expected it—like a legion of devils. There was no simple bargain and treaty possible save unconditional surrender to what they knew not. Call it spirit, call it life, call it the end of all they had once treasured and embraced in blindness and ignorance and obstinacy they knew. They were the pursuers and now they had become the pursued. Indeed it looked the utmost inextricable confusion to determine where they were and what they were, whether they had made any step whatever towards a better relationship—amongst themselves and within themselves—or whether it was all a fantastic chimera.

They stared hopelessly into the air up the high walls and precipice that hung over their head—an ancient familiar house and structure—and as hopelessly into the bright future and sun that streamed. It was all one impossible burden and deterrent they could neither return to nor escape.

They felt themselves broken and finished in the endless nightmare and they slouched and nodded in the stream. Vigilance alone preserved the vessel straight ahead, steering with spider arm and engine. The water grew still and quiet and clear as heaven. The Arawak woman pointed. A dense flock of parrots wheeled and flew and a feather settled on Vigilance's cheek with a breath of life. They wheeled closer and nearer until he saw the white fire of feathers—around their baiting eye, giving them a wise inquisitive expression and look—and the green fire on their bubbling wing as they rose from the stream and the cliff and the sun.

Vigilance had been wounded by a nameless shaft from the enormous unpredictable battlements he dreamed he stormed—cliff and sun and rock and river all set with their ceaseless pursuing trap as if he were the most precious remarkable game in all the world. Nevertheless he was the one most alive and truly aware of everything. He saw differently and felt differently to the way the herd slept in the innocent stream of death. All blind lust and obfuscation had been banished from his mind. Indeed the living life that ran within him was a unique and grotesque privilege and coincidence because of the extraordinary depth and range he now possessed. Vision and idea mingled into a sensitive carnival that turned the crew into the fearful herd where he clung with his eye of compassion to his precarious and dizzy vertical hold and perched on the stream of the cliff. The light of space changed, impinging upon his eyeball and lid numerous grains of sound and motion that were the suns and moons of all space and time. The fowls of the air danced and wheeled on invisible lines that stretched taut between the ages of light and snapped every now and then into lightning executions of dreaming men when each instant ghost repaired the wires again in the form of an inquisitive hanging eye and bird.

The feather on his face pricked him like a little stab of fear as though he had not yet become reconciled to his understanding. He felt himself drawn again into the endless flight that had laid siege to the ambivalent wall of heaven and every spidery misstep he made turned into an intricate horror of space and a falling coincidence and wing. The parrots wheeled and flew around his head on the cliff and the Arawak woman pointed again to a close silver ring that girdled one flying foot. Vigilance rubbed his eye in vain. It was strange but there it was.

"That bird got a ring on he foot," said daSilva, opening one sudden leering dreaming eye, his face all puffed and unnatural in awkward sleep. One could see he was struggling with all the might of his mind to recall something. "I sure-sure I see that bird long ago, sure as dead." He stared fixedly at the creature and shook his head.

"In the London Zoo," Cameron jeered and snored. "Is there you see it and now it fly all the way to Brazil with its pretty ring on its foot to look at you and me. We is a sight for sore eyes. But is where this ring you seeing? I can't see no ring on no bird foot. Is how many ring and vulture you counting in the sky?" He laughed a little, unable however to hide his fear of the beak of death that had been born in his sleep.

"I never been to London or to a zoo," daSilva yawned lugubriously. "And I didn't tell you nothing about vulture. Is parrot Ah seeing and one got a ring on she foot. O God you think I blind or what? How you can't see it I don't know. You mean is another dream Ah dreaming?" He turned wooden and still, speaking almost to himself in the lapping whispers water made against the boat when the wind blew. "Ah been dreaming far far back before anybody know he born. Is how a man can dream so far back before he know he born?" He looked at Cameron with conviction and enquiry in his eye.

"Because you is a big fool," Cameron cried. "A fool of fools. Look at you. You face like a real dead man own. I hungry." He tried to laugh and his tongue was black. "I going nail and drop one of them vulture bird sure as stones. . ." The novel idea seemed to wake nearly all of the crew from boredom and they stared in encouragement as Cameron felt in the bottom for a rock.

"I is a fool yes, a foolish dead man," daSilva puffed, "but I seeing me parrot. Is no vulture bird. . . ."

"What in heaven name really preying on you sight and mind, Boy?" Cameron suddenly became curious. "I only seeing vulture bird. Where the parrot what eating you?"

"Ah telling you Ah dream the boat sink with all of we," daSilva said speaking to himself as if he had forgotten Cameron's presence. "Ah drowned dead and Ah float. All of we expose and float. . ."

"Is vulture bird you really feeling and seeing," shouted Cameron. His voice was a croak in the air. DaSilva continued—a man grown deaf and blind with sleep—"Ah dream Ah get another chance to live me life over from the very start. Live me life over from the very start, you hear?" He paused and the thought sank back into the stream. "The impossible start to happen. Ah lose me own image and time like if I forget is where me sex really start. . . ."

"Fool, stop it," Cameron hissed.

"Don't pick at me," daSilva said. "The impossible start happen I tell you. Water start dream, rock and stone start dream, tree trunk and tree root dreaming, bird and beast dreaming. . . ."

"You is a menagerie and a jungle of a fool," Cameron's black tongue laughed and twisted.

"Everything Ah tell you dreaming long before the creation I know of begin. Everything turning different, changing into everything else Ah tell you. Nothing at all really was there. That is," he grew confused "that is nothing I know of all me life to be something. . ." He stopped at a dead loss for words open mouthed and astonished as if he had been assaulted by the madness and innocence of the stream.

"Tek a batty fool like you to dream that," said Cameron. "A batty fool like you. . ."

"Is a funny-funny dream," daSilva said slowly, recovering himself a little. "To dream all this . . ." he pointed at the wall of cliff behind him—"deh pon you back like nothing, like air standing up. . . ."

"You got a strong-strong back," Cameron croaked and his hands brushed the water with beak and wings.

"Is true," daSilva sulked. His mind grew suddenly startled and punctured as the stream. "I know is who bird now," he gasped and shouted. "I remember clear." He pointed at the parrot and the silver ring with such swamping eagerness and enthusiasm the words drowned on his lips . . . "Is me . . . is mine . . ."

The crew rippled and laughed like water so loud and long that Donne awoke to their merriment.

"What? what is it?" he said.

"Laugh good," daSilva warned. "You going laugh good again like a guest at me true marriage and wedding feast. . . ."

"Must be in heaven," Cameron croaked and roared in Donne's ear.

"Is me lady bird," daSilva insisted. "It must be fly away from she for a morning outing. Them people ain't deh far," he cried in a burst of inspiration. "The lil bird tekking a morning outing . . . I know it. Last year when Ah been with she in the Mission Ah feed it meself often. It used to eat from me lip. Tame Ah tell you. Is me mistress bird." He whistled.

"It's good news then," said Donne. "Yesterday we witnessed the huntsman's promissory wound and today daSilva's promissory ring . . ." he laughed. "The folk are close at hand to save us." He did not believe a word he said in his heart and he added a warning note—"Of course you chaps mustn't bank on anything too much. A bird like that can fly a hundred miles in an hour. Still we must hope for the best." He smiled stiffly, waving his hand darkly to greet the air.

"I feed it often from me lip," daSilva said whistling loud. "Me pretty lady bird. She and me was one flesh. I going marry she this time Ah tell you.

Look she leg slender. Slender like . . . like . . ." he stared unseeingly . . . "a branch . . ." he was uncertain.

"Like poison," said Cameron.

"Slender branch," said daSilva as if he was drunk. "And she taste sweet. Me mistress breasts like sweet cocerite. She got sweet-sweet honey lip too. And she hair long and black like midnight feathers. Ah kiss she eyes fast and thick till she nearly dead in me hand. . ."

"What a vulture of a bird you are," Cameron grinned in derision ."You never speak a truer word than when you say you got everything mix up in you head. . ." He had hardly stopped speaking when he flung a stone and bird past Jennings's head. Aimlessly. The crew gave a sudden answering cry. The stone had cut air and flesh and it fell. But on fluttering upon the water it recovered itself instantly and wings flashed and soared. The whole flock rose in swelling protest higher and higher until all dwindled in the sky at the top of the wall.

"Miss," Cameron cried.

"You wounded it," Donne said quietly. "We have given ourselves away as their huntsman gave them away. O never mind I'm sure I'm talking nonsense. I can't see a thing."

"I used to feed it from me lip," daSilva whimpered.

"O shut up," Cameron waved. "What do you mean—give ourselves away?" he asked.

"O well," said Donne speaking without conviction, "the bird may return bleeding with a mark upon it. The folk may take it in their heart to start hunting us. We can never outwit them now. Our strength is gone. Three of our best men finished. No ammunition. Nothing remaining. Everything overboard. We can only throw imaginary stones in the air to frighten and alarm ourselves and make imaginary rings in the water. . ."

"Better we stop and turn back," said Jennings sombrely.

"Impossible. Where can we land? If we turn back we're lost. How can we run the rapids in our condition? We do need help more than ever to locate a safe ground trail if we succeed in escaping these walls . . ." he waved his hands at the cliff. "O it's a hellish business and trial and responsibility I never foresaw. If one of us—" he stared at them with a glassy eye—"gets across he'll carry the mark of a beast or a bird I tell you. It's a wounding dream and task . . ." he began to ramble and rave. "Let's hope there'll be someone there to meet us and heal us in the end whatever we are. It's all that counts. . . ."

"Ah used to feed she with me lip," daSilva said.

"O shut up," Cameron cried. "Who cares?"

"Why did you pelt it?" daSilva cried.

"Wait you going on like if is you I pelt. Aw shut up, I hungry."

"I ask you why you pelt the ring of me flesh. . ."

"O Christ, shut up," said Cameron. "I didn't pelt *you*. I didn't see no precious ring. You is bewitched . . . that's what. . ."

DaSilva muttered wildly—"I tell you when you pelt she you pelt me. Is one flesh, me flesh, you flesh, one flesh. She come to save me, to save all of we. You murderer! what else is you but a plain vile murderer? She ain't no witch. . . ." His face was mad.

"Who say she is a witch, . . ." Cameron began to protest.

DaSilva jumped. Cameron's hands flashed. For the first time in his life he missed. The truth was he had no footing in the water: he groaned and fell, his face grinning and splashing surprise. The crew were dumb. They bore him up unwittingly. He was dead and his blood ran and encircled their hand.

DaSilva shook like a leaf. The knife and blade fell from his fingers as flesh from bone turning clean and silver in the stream.

"O God," said Donne in voiceless surprise and horror as at himself. "What have you done daSilva to a bosom friend?"

DaSilva did not hear and understand. He too was deaf and dumb. He saw Cameron in the stream and in the sky where their joint flesh had flown and darted above the fantasy of their carnal death. He looked around foolishly, telling himself Cameron had attacked him in some idle and faithless fashion. It all seemed blind and empty now like the air and stream that jostled them.

The Arawak woman pointed and Vigilance, straining his mind from the volcanic precipice where he clung, looked and saw the blue ring of pentecostal fire in God's eye as it wheeled around him above the dreaming memory and prison of life until it melted where neither wound nor witch stood.

9

The Arawak woman rolled like a ball on the cliff, clinging to tree and stone and Vigilance was able to follow. The river crept far beneath them, and above them—beyond the wall they were climbing—lay safety and freedom. Vigilance knew that every step he made was a miracle of survival. It was incredible he had escaped after the wreck of the boat and succeeded in climbing so far and high. Millions of years had passed he knew until now he felt bruised and wounded beyond words and his limbs had crawled and still flew. He had slept in a cradle of branches and in a cave overlooking the chasm of time. However strange it was the fact remained he was living after all. The memory of the conventional crew was a dead eccentric belief that still continued to haunt him every now and then whenever he thought he had fallen and died in the primitive moments of a universal emptiness and fear.

The fantasy of the fourth day dawned—the fourth day of creation—since they had all set out from Mariella. From his godlike perch he discerned the image of the musing boat in which they had come. They had found a cave the previous nightfall and they had stretched their limbs until morning.

It was a close fit lying there—too close for ease and normal sleep—and everyone stirred when Vigilance moved. They could not help turning their dull eye upon the vessel they had managed to anchor at their ghostly side in the stream and it was as if they sought a long lost friend and soul. Everyone stirred and woke, all except Cameron. He was dead with a stab wound in his back. In their enormous fatigue the night and day before they had kept him at their side as they would an idol and companion.

They hurriedly abandoned him in the cliff, turning the room in which they had slept into his grave alone, and were soon travelling fast in the river when Jennings deliberately shut off the engine and the boat swung in the stream, lodging its bow in a fresh hollow of stone.

"Ah got an idea," he announced. He spoke with hopeless obstinacy. His face was no longer the same as before: it had changed into a dream, the dream of an unnatural unshaven dead man's beard and growth. The cheeks were hollow as the caves in the wall and the blackness of his skin had grown lighter and greyer into an older drier mask and presence lying within. The lust and soul of rebellion had been killed abruptly in a manner that left him suddenly empty. He felt now only the loss of an opposition and true adversary within himself. His eyes had lost all rude fire and in their blindness and loneliness they spun deeper than nature's darkness and light. It was the strangest abstract face Vigilance had ever seen—the abstraction of a shell afloat over a propeller and a machine with the consistency of a duty rather than of a desire and a spirit. Indeed it reminded him of a coconut shell he had once observed beached against the river; someone had brought it a long way from its natural grave on the seacoast and deposited it here dry and desiccated and foreign in the midst of the river's stone and vegetation. He had held the husk in his hand and it had given a dry brittle harp's cry of relief, mummified and mystical and Egyptian, melting at the same time into an inner dust that crumbled to an ancient door of life.

It was the oldest soulless expression of self-surrender he had ever seen—the dutiful mask of resurrection and the engineer of death.

"Ah got an idea," said Jennings again. His voice was meaningless. "Let we look for the hole where the wild tapir pass through the cliff. Was when? Yesterday? Or day before yesterday? Let we pass through the same door to the land. . . This is dead man river. . . We can't stay here any more. . . ."

DaSilva shook his head. "Ah dream you done dead already Jennings," he tried to crack a joke. "And the hole close up for good for you a million year ago. You is a prehistoric animal." His chest brayed foolishly. "Where Cameron?" he asked.

No one replied.

"Where Cameron?" he asked again. A sickly smile that reflected everyone's condemnation wrinkled his lips. "Ah dream Cameron dead too," he confessed, "and yet he swim and float next to me trying to hug me and kiss me. Is he pull me down. Is a sight to feel a drowning man clinging to you," he pleaded and confessed. "I had to stab at he to mek he loose me. And still he hold on. Don't mind how ugly you find it . . ." he shuddered and hiccoughed in a sentimental bloated fashion of goodwill, . . . "is still the dream of love floating everywhere . . . I forgive he . . . even if he mek me dream bad that a bewitched whore killed us both . . . grabbed hold us in the water . . . pulled us down. . ." He spoke with the blind innocence of a clown floundering in the blank of memory in the shattering of his life.

Jennings turned his abstract face towards him indifferently as if he knew another version. "Yes is common knowledge you kill poor Cameron daSilva. Is common knowledge in the world you encourage he to mek this trip and that you quarrel stupid-stupid with he in the end. Nobody know the reason 'cept was jealousy or love. Is he probe at me till he enrage me to lef' the shit I been living in. I was always a stay-at-home not like wutless Cammy." A grotesque tear opened his cheek.

DaSilva chuckled gaining a flash of an old rumour of fellowship in winning this ugly tear and response —"He butt me like if he was mad. I dive and pull away from he. . . But I didn't mean to hurt he. Not Cammy. How could I ever hurt Cammy? Was me last memory and hope of happiness in this world. I remember feeling surprised that I had seconds of drowning life and fight lef' in me while poor Cammy was bewildered and dead and didn't feel a thing. . . ."

"You believe a drown-man skin got no feeling in it and can't make out friend or foe pon his back?" Jennings mumbled his rhetorical senseless question and his face cracked open a little more. He knew it was all invention, daSilva's erratic memory and story, all the crude prevarication and sentiment of life they debated and that it was pointless and pretentious for one dead man (which was the only feeling he felt inside himself) to address another on non-existent spiritual and emotional facts. No one could truly discern a reason and a motive and a distinction in anything. It was as bad as talking of two sexes and of blind love all in the same breath in his wife's mother's sitting-room. The old harridan! she had helped to drive him from his hell and his home. The shock of memory and of a duty to fight to rescue himself drove him again to address himself to the thought of another frightful revolution and escape he had to engineer however soulless and devastating the thought of a living return to the world was.

"If we find the door where the wild tapir pass we can land and live. . ." He spoke without conviction and with dread at the thought of embarking again for a place he hardly relished and knew. It was better to stay just where he was and crumble inwardly he said like a man who had come back to his shell of nothingness and functional beginning again.

"What tapir?" mocked daSilva. "I tell you I remember no tapir. You recall any?" He turned in a foolish mocking way to his twin brother.

Vigilance was startled. He had forgotten this particular twin and brother. He recalled seeing him last with Donne tracking the old woman in the Mission while the other one remained with Cameron at the campfire. He had completely forgotten him until now when he saw him in the mirror of the dreaming soul again—an artifice of flight that had been summoned rather than a living man and way of escape. His reflection was the frailest shadow of a former self. His bones were splinters and points Vigilance saw and his flesh was newspaper, drab, wet until the lines and markings had run fantastically together. His hair stood flat on his brow like ink. He nodded precariously and one marvelled how he preserved his appearance without disintegrating into soggy lumps and patches when the wind blew and rocked the pins of his bones a little. He shook his head again but not a word blew from his lips. DaSilva stared at the apparition his brother presented as a man would stare at a reporter who had returned from the grave with no news whatsoever of a living return.

Now he knew for the first true time the fetishes he and his companions had embraced. They were bound together in wishful substance and in the very enormity of a dreaming enmity and opposition and self-destruction. Remove all this or weaken its appearance and its cruelty and they were finished. So Donne had died in the death of Wishrop; Jennings's primitive abstraction and slackening will was a reflection of the death of Cameron, Schomburgh had died with Carroll. And daSilva saw with dread his own sogging fool's life on the threshold of the ultimate stab of discredit like one who had adventured and lived on scraps of vulgar intention and detection and rumour that passed for the arrest of spiritual myth and the rediscovery of a new life in the folk.

Vigilance dreamed and felt all this; he recognised the total exhaustion of his companions like his own superstitious life and limbs. And he rested against the wall and cliff of heaven as against an indestructible mirror and soul in which he saw the blind dream of creation crumble as it was re-enacted.

BOOK IV

Paling of Ancestors

This piece-bright paling shuts the spouse
Christ home, Christ and his mother and all his hallows.

HOPKINS

10

The daSilva twin and scarecrow of death had vanished in the dawn of the fifth day. Donne rubbed his eyes in astonishment. He did not feel inclined to search every cave and indentation in the wall, and after a lusty shout and halloo brought no reply, he decided to set out again and go on. Furthermore Vigilance and the old Arawak woman had also disappeared. Donne rubbed his eyes again wondering whether on leaving Cameron in the cave the previous day he had lost count of the living crew as well. An idea flashed upon him and he scanned the smooth cliff as if he followed a reflection. He saw nothing, however. And a wave of hopelessness enveloped him: everyone in the vessel was crumbling into a door into the sun through which one perceived nothing standing—the mirror of absolute nothingness.

An abstraction grew around him—nothing else—the ruling abstraction of himself which he saw reflected nowhere. He was a ruler of men and a ruler of nothing. The sun rose into the blinding wall and river before him filling the stream and water with melting gold. He dipped his hand in but nothing was there.

He felt it was certainly better to move than remain where he was, and he started the engine, pointing the boat up-river for the fifth morning and time. Jennings's wrist was aching and swollen. Donne sent him to serve as look-out at the bow while daSilva remained between them, in the middle, smiling foolishly at nothing.

The river was calm as the day before, innocent and golden as a dream. The boat ran smoothly until the stream seemed to froth and bubble a little against it. A change was at hand in the sky of water everyone sensed and knew. The vessel seemed to hasten and the river grew black, painted with streaks of a foaming white. The noise of a thunderous waterfall began to dawn on their ear above the voice of their engine. They saw in the distance at last a thread of silver lightning that expanded and grew into a veil of smoke. They drew as near as they could and stopped under the cloud. Right and left grew the universal wall of cliff they knew, and before them the highest waterfall they had ever seen moved and still stood upon the escarpment. They were plainly astonished at the immaculate bridal veil falling motionlessly from the river's tall brink. The cliffs appeared to box and imprison the waterfall. A light curious fern grew out of the stone, and pearls were burning and smoking from the greenest brightest dwarfs and trees they remembered.

Steps and balconies had been nailed with abandon from bottom to top making hazardous ladders against the universal walls. These were wreathed in misty arms blowing from the waterfall.

Donne looked at the engine and felt its work was finished. They needed only their bare dreaming hands and feet now to climb the wall. He unscrewed it from its hold and wedged it at the foot of the musing stairway. Jennings and daSilva assisted him also in hauling the boat out of the water and upon a flat stone. In a couple of months it would start to rot in the sun like a drowned man's hulk in the abstraction of a day and an age. As he bade good-bye to it—as to another faithful companion—he knew there was some meaning in his farewell sadness, something that had duration and value beyond the years of apparent desertion and death, but it baffled him and slipped away from him. All he knew was the misty sense of devastating thoroughness, completion and endless compassion—so far-reaching and distant and all-embracing and still remote, it amounted to nothingness again.

He shook himself into hands and feet of quicksilver and dream and started his ascent of the ladder, followed painfully by Jennings and daSilva.

As he made the first step the memory of the house he had built in the savannahs returned to him with the closeness and intimacy of a horror and a hell, that horror and that hell he had himself elaborately constructed from which to rule his earth. He ascended higher, trying to shake away his obsession. He slipped and gasped on the misty step and a noose fell around his neck from which he dangled until—after an eternity—he had regained a breathless footing. The shock made him dizzy—the mad thought he had been supported by death and nothingness. It flashed on him looking down the steep spirit of the cliff that this dreaming return to a ruling function of nothingness and to a false sense of home was the meaning of hell. He stared upward to heaven slowly as to a new beginning from which the false hell and function crumbled and fell.

A longing swept him like the wind of the muse to understand and transform his beginnings: to see the indestructible nucleus and redemption of creation, the remote and the abstract image and correspondence, in which all things and events gained their substance and universal meaning. However far from him, however distant and removed, he longed to see, *he longed to see* the atom, the very nail of moment in the universe. It would mean more to him than an idol of idols even if in seeing it there was frustration in that the distance between himself and *It* strengthened rather than weakened. The frustration would disappear he knew in his sense of a new functional inspiration and beginning and erection in living nature and scaffolding.

The wind rushed down the cliff so strong he almost fell again but it turned and braced him at last and he continued ascending as a workman in the heart and on the face of construction. He fastened on this notion to keep his mind from slipping. The roaring water was a droning misty machine, and the hammer of the fall shook the earth with the misty blow of fate. A swallow flew and dashed through the veil and window. His eyes darted from his head and Donne saw a young carpenter in a room. A light shone from the roof and the curtains wreathed slowly. Donne tried to attract the young man's attention but he did not hear and understand his summons. He hammered against the wall and shook the window loud. Everything quietly resisted. The young carpenter nevertheless turned his face to him at last and looked through him outside. His eyes were darker than the image of the sky and the swallow that had flown towards him was reflected in them as in window-panes of glass. Donne flattened himself against the wall until his nose had been planed down to his face. He wanted to see the carpenter closely and to draw his attention. He saw the chisel in his hand and the saw and hammer lying on the table while the ground was strewn with shavings resembling twigs and leaves. A rectangular face it was, chiselled and cut from the cedar of Lebanon. He was startled and frightened by the fleshless wood, the lips a breath apart full of grains from the skeleton of a leaf on the ground branching delicately and sensitively upward into the hair on his head that parted itself in the middle and fell on both sides of his face into a harvest. His fingers were of the same wood, the nails made of bark and ivory. Every movement and glance and expression was a chiselling touch, the divine alienation and translation of flesh and blood into everything and anything on earth. The chisel was old as life, old as a finger-nail. The saw was the teeth of bone. Donne felt himself sliced with this skeleton-saw by the craftsman of God in the window-pane of his eye. The swallow flew in and out like a picture on the wall framed by the carpenter to breathe perfection.

He began hammering again louder than ever to draw the carpenter's intimate attention. He had never felt before such terrible desire and frustration all mingled. He knew the chisel and the saw in the room had touched him and done something in the wind and the sun to make him anew. Finger-nail and bone were secret panes of glass in the stone of blood through which spiritual eyes were being opened. He felt these implements of vision operating upon him, and still he had no hand to hold anything tangible and no voice loud enough to address anyone invisible. But the carpenter still stood plain before him in the room with the picture of the swallow on the wall perfectly visible amidst all and everything, and there was no earthly excuse why he could not reach him. He hammered again loud to attract his attention, the kind of attention and appreciation dead habit taught him to desire. The carpenter still looked through him as through the far-seeing image and constellation of his eye—clouds and star and sun on the window-panes. He hammered again but nothing broke the distance between them. It was as if he looked into a long dead room in which the carpenter was sealed and immured for good. Time had no meaning. The room was as old as a cave and as new as a study. The walls—whether of glass or stone or wood—were thicker than the stratosphere. All sound had been barred and removed for ever, all communication, all persuasion, all intercourse. It was Death with capitals, and when he saw this he felt too that it was he who stood within the room and it was the carpenter who stood reflected without. This was a fantasy, this change of places, and he hammered again loud. The image of Death in the carpenter stared through him, the eyelids flickered with lightning at last in the midst of the waterfall.

He raised his hammer and struck the blow that broke every spell. Donne quivered and shook like a dead branch whose roots were reset on their living edge.

The carpenter turned to another picture he had framed on the wall. An animal was bounding towards him through the prehistoric hole in the cliff Jennings had dreamed to find. It had a wound in its side from a spear and its great horns curved into a crescent moon as if the very spear had been turned and bent.

The animal was so lithe and swift one had no eye for anything else. It bounded and glanced everywhere, on the table, on the windowsill with the dying light of the sun, drawing itself together into a musing ball. It danced around the room swift as running light, impetuous as a dream. It was everywhere and nowhere, a picture of abandonment and air, a cat on crazy balls of feet. It was the universe whose light turned in the room to signal the approach of evening, painting the carpenter's walls with shades from the sky—the most elaborate pictures and seasons he stored and framed and imagined. The room grew crowded with visions he planed and chiselled and nailed into his mind, golden sights, the richest impressions of eternity. It was a millionaire's room—the carpenter's. He touched the dying animal light at last as it ran past him and it turned its head around towards him, a little startled by his alien fingers and hand, remembering something forgotten. The alert dreaming skin—radiant with spiritual fear and ecstasy—quivered and vibrated like the strings of a harp where the mark of the old wound was and it tossed the memory of the spear on its head, trying to recall the miracle of substance and flesh. It stood thus—with the carpenter's hand upon it—with a curious abstract and wooden memory of its life and its death. The sense of death was a wooden dream, a dream of music in the sculptured ballet of the leaves and the seasons, the shavings on the ground from the carpenter's saw and chisel. His finger had touched an ancient spear point and branch and splinter and nail, whose nervous vibration summoned a furious portrait to be framed by the memory of creation. The window-pane clouded a little with the mist of falling evening and water and one had to press one's face and rub with all one's might to see through. The animal light body and wound—upon which his hand lay—turned into an outline of time followed by its own wild reflection vague and enormous as the sky crowding the room. The bulb shining from the roof turned green as water, weird and beautiful as the light-colour from long-dead twinkling stars and suns millions of years old. The room became a dancing hieroglyph in the illumination of endless pursuit, the subtle running depths of the sea, the depths of the green sky and the depths of the forest. It was the mist on the window-pane of the carpenter's room, and one had to rub furiously to see.

One saw a comet tailing into a flock of anxious birds before the huntsman of death who stood winding his horn in the waterfall. Swift as a spear, each one's fear flew plunging into their own outline and stream and side. The sky turned into a running deer and ram, half-ram, half-deer running for life. A catastrophic image of fear and a cloud of speed it was, awkward and uncouth like a mad goat. A ball of wind was set in motion on the cliff. Leaves sprang up from nowhere, a stampede of ghostly men and women all shaped by the leaves, raining and running against the sky.

They besieged the walls of the carpenter's room, clamouring and hammering with the waterfall. He leaned down and removed the dreaming shaft once again from the side of the hunted ram—as he had moved it an eternity before—and restored the bent spear of the new moon where it belonged. The signs of tumult died in the animal light and cloud and the stars only thronged everywhere. So bright they framed his shape through the misty window-panes. The carpenter looked blind to the stumbling human darkness that still trailed and followed across the world. He closed his window softly upon Donne and Jennings and daSilva.

Jennings cried slipping suddenly in the dark upon a step in the cliff. His wrist gave way too with the shaft of his dreaming engine snapping at last as a branch in the flight of the stream. They both answered him but their voices were drowned in the waterfall and they saw nothing save the ancient winding horn of the moon falling from the sky like the bone of his metal and wood.

They shook with the primitive ram again, scanning the endless cliff in fear and ecstasy, feeling for the bodily image of themselves.

Darkness still fell upon the cliff and the horn of the new moon vanished in the end behind the window of the wall as into a long-feared shelter in the earth rich with the frames of humility of God's memory and reflection. The stars in the sky shivered as they crawled once more up the fantastic ladder and into the void of themselves. They wondered whose turn would be next to fall from the sky as the last ghost of the crew had died and they alone were left to frame Christ's tree and home.

As they climbed upward Donne felt the light shine on him reflected from within. He had come upon another window in the wall. The curtains were drawn a little and after he had rubbed the window-panes he began to make out the interior of the room. He looked for the carpenter but at first he saw no one. And then it grew on him a woman was standing within. A child also stood at her feet seeming hardly above her knee. The room was an enormous picture. It breathed all burning tranquillity and passion together—so alive—so warm and true—Donne cried and rapped with the world of his longing. He felt a glowing intimacy as he knocked but the distance between himself and the frame stood as the distance between himself and the stars.

The room was as simple as the carpenter's room. Indeed as he looked he could not help reflecting it was simpler still. Bare, unfurnished, save for a crib in a stall that might have been an animal's trough. Yet it all looked so remarkable—every thread and straw on the ground, the merest touch in the woman's smile and dress—that the light of the room turned into the wealth of dreams.

The woman was dressed in a long sweeping garment belonging to a far and distant age. She wore it so absent-mindedly and naturally however that one could not help being a little puzzled by it. The truth was it was threadbare. One felt that a false move from her would bring it tumbling to the ground. When she walked however it still remained on her back as if it was made of the lightest shrug of her shoulders—all threads of light and fabric from the thinnest strongest source of all beginning and undying end.

The whole room reflected this threadbare glistening garment. The insubstantial straw in the cradle, the skeleton line of boards made into an animal's trough, the gleaming outline of the floor and the wall, and the shift the child wore standing against the woman's knee—all were drawn with such slenderness and everlasting impulse one knew it was richer than all the images of seduction combined to the treasuries of the east. Nothing could match this spirit of warmth and existence. Staring into the room —willing to be blinded—he suddenly saw what he had missed before. The light in the room came from a solitary candle with a star upon it, steady and unflinching, and the candle stood tall and rooted in the floor as the woman was. She moved at last and her garment brushed against it like hair that neither sparked nor flew. He stared and saw her astonishing face. Not a grain of her dress but shone with her hair, clothing her threadbare limbs in the melting plaits of herself. Her ancient dress was her hair after all, falling to the ground and glistening and waving until it grew so frail and loose and endless, the straw in the cradle entered and joined it and the whole room was enveloped in it as a melting essence yields itself and spreads itself from the topmost pinnacle and star into the roots of self and space.

Donne knew he was truly blind now at last. He saw nothing. The burning pain he felt suddenly in his eye extended down his face and along the column of his neck until it branched into nerves and limbs. His teeth loosened in their sockets and he moved his tongue gingerly along them. He trembled as he saw himself inwardly melting into nothingness and into the body of his death. He kept sliding on the slippery moss of the cliff and along columns and grease and mud. A singular thought always secured him to the scaffolding. It was the unflinching clarity with which he looked into himself and saw that all his life he had loved no one but himself. He focused his blind eye with all penitent might on this pinpoint star and reflection as one looking into the void of oneself upon the far greater love and self-protection that have made the universe.

The stars shivered again as they climbed. The night was cold, ice-cold and yet on fire. His blindness began melting and soon had burned away from him, he thought, though he knew this was impossible He had entered the endless void of himself and the stars were invisible. He was blind. He accepted every invisible light and conceived it as an intimate and searching reflection which he was helping to build with each step he made. His unique eye was a burning fantasy he knew. He was truly blind. He saw nothing, he saw the unselfness of night, the invisible otherness around, the darkness all the time, he saw the stars he knew to be invisible however much they appeared to shine above him. He saw an enormity of sky which was as alien to him as flesh to wood. He saw something but he had not grasped it. It was his blindness that made him see his own nothingness and imagination constructed beyond his reach.

This was the creation and reflection he shared with another and leaned upon as upon one frame that stood—free from material restraint and possession—as the light and life of dead or living stars whom no one beheld for certain in the body of their death or their life. They were a ghost of light and that was all. The void of themselves alone was real and structural. All else was dream borrowing its light from a dark invisible source akin to human blindness and imagination that looked through nothingness all the time to the spirit that had secured life. Step by step up the support grew and contained everything with a justness and exactness as true to life as a spark of fire lived, and with an unyielding motive that crumbled material age and idolatry alike.

They were exhausted after a long while, and they leaned in a doorway of the night hammering in blindness and frustration with the fist of the waterfall. They had been able to lay hold upon nothing after all. It was finished and they fell.

The door they hammered upon was the face of

the earth itself where they lay. It swung wide at last with the brunt of the wind. The dawn had come, the dawn of the sixth day of creation. The sun rose in a cloud hinged to the sky. DaSilva stood within the door in the half-shadow. He looked old and finished and beaten to death after his great fall. Donne stared at him with nervous horror and fascination and in his mind he knew he was dead. He could see nothing and yet he dreamt he saw everything clearer than ever before. DaSilva was opening the door again to him: hands stiff and outstretched and foolishly inviting him to step into the empty hall. His mouth gaped in a smile and his teeth protruded half-broken and smashed. The high bones still stood in his face as when he had signalled their downfall. The early sun climbed a little higher and the world beneath the cliff became an aerial portrait framed in mist. The river shone clear as glass and a pinpoint started glittering in the bed of the stream. The mist rolled away from the cliff and the sun curled and tossed a lioness mane that floated slowly up into the sky over the dead. The resurrection head was uplifted and the great body rolled over in a blanket. DaSilva was shivering and shaking cold as death. Indeed he had never been so bitterly cold. He had woken to find himself inside the house and Donne hammering away outside almost in a heap together at the bottom of the wall.

He had fumbled for the catch and release in the door, trembling and astonished at himself. The great cliff sprang open like the memory of the lion's spring he had made tumbling him smashed and broken on the ground. Every bone seemed to break and he wrapped himself in the misery of death. But the wind that had sprung upon him flew out again shaking him from his blanket on the ground.

It was strange to wake to the world the first morning he had died he told himself a little foolishly. Donne was standing on the threshold staring blind and mad. DaSilva smiled crookedly because he felt that Donne thought he was dead. He knew better and he stretched out his hand. Donne mumbled to him like a man saying a prayer. . . .

"It is better to be a doorkeeper in the house of the Lord . . ." he mumbled foolishly. He stepped over the eloquent arms that reached to him in a fixation of greeting. DaSilva was dead he knew. He entered the corridor over the dead body and stood himself at strict attention by the lion door. He had stopped a little to wonder whether he was wrong in his knowledge and belief and the force that had divided them from each other—and mangled them beyond all earthly hope and recognition—was the wind of rumour and superstition, and the truth was they had all come home at last to the compassion of the nameless unflinching folk.

11

It was the seventh day from Mariella. And the creation of the windows of the universe was finished. Vigilance stood at the top of the sky he had gained at last following the muse of love, and I looked over his dreaming shoulder into the savannahs that reached far away into the morning everywhere. The sun rolled in the grasses waving in the wind and grew on the solitary tree. It was a vast impression and canvas of nature wherein everything looked perfect and yet at the same time unfinished and insubstantial. One had an intuitive feeling that the savannahs—though empty—were crowded. A metaphysical outline dwelt everywhere filling in blocks where spaces stood and without this one would never have perceived the curious statement of completion and perfection. The work was truly finished but no one would have known it or seen it or followed it without a trusting kinship and contagion.

The eye and window through which I looked stood now in the dreaming forehead at the top of the cliff in the sky. The grave demeanour of cattle and sheep roamed everywhere in the future of distance, lurking in pencils and images of cloud and sun and leaf. Horsemen—graven signs of man and beast—stood at attention melting and constant like water running on a pane of glass. The sun grew higher still and the fluid light turned and became a musical passage—a dark corridor and summons and call in the network of the day. We stood there—our eye and shoulder profound and retiring—feeling for the shadow of our feet on the ground. The light rolled and burned into quicksilver and hair shining in the window of my eye until it darkened. I found the courage to make my first blind wooden step. Like the step of the tree in the distance. My feet were truly alive I realized, as were my dreaming shoulder and eye; as far flung and distant from me as a man in fever thinks his thumb to be removed from his fingers; far away as heaven's hand. It was a new sensation and alien body and experience encompassing the ends of the earth. I had started to walk at last—after a long infancy and dreaming death—in the midst of mutilation and chaos that had no real power to overcome me. Rather I felt it was the unique window through which I now looked that supported the life of nature and gave it a full and invisible meaning and perfection in the way I knew my hands and feet were formed and supported at this instant.

I had never before looked on the blinding world in this trusting manner—through an eye I shared only with the soul, the soul and mother of the universe. Across the crowded creation of the invisible savannahs the newborn wind of spirit blew the sun making light of everything, curious hands and feet, neck, shoulder, forehead, material twin shutter and eye. They drifted, half-finished sketches in the air, until they were filled suddenly from within to become living and alive. I saw the tree in the distance wave its arms and walk when I looked at it through the spiritual eye of the soul. First it shed its leaves sudden and swift as if the gust of the wind that blew had ripped it almost bare. The bark and wood turned to lightning flesh and the sun which had been suspended from its head rippled and broke into stars that stood where the shattered leaves had been in the living wake of the storm. The enormous starry dress it now wore spread itself all around into a full majestic gown from which emerged the intimate column of a musing neck, face and hands, and twinkling feet. The stars became peacocks' eyes, and the great tree of flesh and blood swirled into another stream that sparkled with divine feathers where the neck and the hands and the feet had been nailed.

This was the palace of the universe and the windows of the soul looked out and in. The living eyes in the crested head were free to observe the twinkling stars and eyes and windows on the rest of the body and the wings. Every cruel mark and stripe and ladder had vanished. I saw a face at one of the other constructions and windows from my observation tower. It was the face of one of the dreaming crew that had died. Carroll, I said, nudging my shoulder, as one would address an oracle for confirmation. Carroll was whistling. A solemn and beautiful cry —unlike a whistle I reflected—deeper and mature. Nevertheless his lips were framed to whistle and I could only explain the difference by assuming the sound from his lips was changed when it struck the window and issued into the world. It was an organ cry almost and yet quite different I reflected again. It seemed to break and mend itself always—tremulous, forlorn, distant, triümphant, the echo of sound so pure and outlined in space it broke again into a mass of music. It was the cry of the peacock and yet I reflected far different. I stared at the whistling lips and wondered if the change was in me or in them. I had never witnessed and heard such sad and such glorious music. I saw a movement and flutter at another window in the corner of my eye like a feather. It was Schomburgh's white head. He too was listening rapt and intent. And I knew now that the music was not an hallucination. He listened too, like me. I saw he was free to listen and to hear at last without fearing a hoax. He stood at his window and I stood at mine, transported beyond the memory of words.

The dark notes rose everywhere, so dark, so sombre, they broke·into a fountain—light as the rainbow—sparkling and immaterial as invisible sources and echoes. The savannahs grew lonely as the sea and broke again into a wave and forest. Tall trees with black marching boots and feet were clad in the spurs and sharp wings of a butterfly. They flew and vanished in the sky with a sound that was terrible and wonderful; it was sorrowful and it was mystical. It spoke with the inner longing of woman and the deep mastery of man. Frail and nervous and yet strong and grounded. And it seemed to me as I listened I had understood that no living ear on earth can truly understand the fortune of love and the art of victory over death without mixing blind joy and sadness and the sense of being lost with the nearness of being found. Carroll whistled to all who had lost love in the world. This was his humorous whimsical sadness.

I was suddenly aware of other faces at other windows in the Palace of the Peacock. And it seemed to me that Carroll's music changed in the same instant. I nudged the oracle of my dreaming shoulder. The change and variation I thought I detected in the harmony were outward and unreal and illusory:

they were induced by the limits and apprehensions in the listening mind of men, and by their wish and need in the world to provide a material nexus to bind the spirit of the universe.

It was this tragic bond I perceived now—as I had felt and heard the earlier distress of love. I listened again intently to the curious distant echo and dragging chain of response outside my window. Indeed this was a unique frame I well knew now to construct the events of all appearance and tragedy into the vain prison they were, a child's game of a besieged and a besieging race who felt themselves driven to seek themselves—first, outcast and miserable twins of fate—second, heroic and warlike brothers—third, conquerors and invaders of all mankind. In reality the territory they overwhelmed and abandoned had always been theirs to rule and take.

Wishrop's face dawned on my mind like the soul of all. He was obviously torn and captivated by Carroll's playing that lifted him out of his mystical conceit. I felt the new profound tone of irony and understanding he possessed, the spirit that allowed him to see himself as he once lived and pretended he was, and at the same time to grasp himself as he now was and had always been—truly nothing in himself.

The wall that had divided him from his true otherness and possession was a web of dreams. His feet climbed a little and they danced again, and the music of the peacock turned him into a subtle step and waltz like the grace and outspread fan of desire that had once been turned by the captain of the crew into a compulsive design and a blind engine of war. His feet marched again as a spider's toward eternity, and the music he followed welled and circumnavigated the globe. The sadness of the song grew heart-rending when he fell and collapsed though his eye still sparkled as a wishing glass in the sun—his flashing teeth and smile—a whistling devil-may-care wind and cry, a ribald outburst that wooed the mysterious cross and substance of the muse Carroll fed to him like the diet of nerve and battle to induce him to find his changeless fortress and life. It was a prodigal web and ladder he held out to him that he climbed again and again in the world's longing voice and soul with his muted steps and stops.

12

The windows of the palace were crowded with faces. I had plainly seen Carroll and Wishrop; and now as plainly I saw Cameron, the adversary of Jennings. I saw as well the newspaper face and twin of the daSilvas who had vanished before the fifth day from Mariella after making an ominous report and appearance. The music Carroll sang and played and whistled suddenly filled the corridors and the chosen ornaments of the palace; I knew it came from a far source within—deeper than every singer knew. And Carroll himself was but a small mouthpiece and echo standing at the window and reflecting upon the world.

In the rooms of the palace where we firmly stood —free from the chains of illusion we had made without—the sound that filled us was unlike the link of memory itself. It was the inseparable moment within ourselves of all fulfilment and understanding. Idle now to dwell upon and recall anything one had ever responded to with the sense and sensibility that were our outward manner and vanity and conceit.

One was what I am in the music—buoyed and supported above dreams by the undivided soul and anima in the universe from whom the word of dance and creation first came, the command to the starred peacock who was instantly transported to know and to hug to himself his true invisible otherness and opposition, his true alien spiritual love without cruelty and confusion in the blindness and frustration of desire. It was the dance of all fulfilment I now held and knew deeply, cancelling my forgotten fear of strangeness and catastrophe in a destitute world.

This was the inner music and voice of the peacock I suddenly encountered and echoed and sang as I had never heard myself sing before. I felt the face before me begin to fade and part company from me and from themselves as if our need of one another was now fulfilled, and our distance from each other was the distance of a sacrament, the sacrament and embrace we knew in one muse and one undying soul. Each of us now held at last in his arms what he had been for ever seeking and what he had eternally possessed.